William H.G. Kingston

Clara Maynard

William H.G. Kingston

Clara Maynard

ISBN/EAN: 9783337062422

Printed in Europe, USA, Canada, Australia, Japan

Cover: Foto ©Raphael Reischuk / pixelio.de

More available books at **www.hansebooks.com**

CLARA MAYNARD;

OR,

THE TRUE AND THE FALSE.

CLARA MAYNARD;

OR

The True and the False.

A TALE OF THE TIMES.

BY

W. H. G. KINGSTON,

AUTHOR OF

"Peter the Whaler," "The Three Midshipmen," "Milicent's Diary,"
"Roger Kyffin's Ward," "The Last Look," etc.

FOURTH THOUSAND.

London:

HODDER AND STOUGHTON,

27, PATERNOSTER ROW.

—

MDCCCLXXIX.

CLARA MAYNARD;

OR,

TRUE AND FALSE.

Chapter I.

THE blue waters of the British Channel sparkled brightly in the rays of the sun, shining forth from a cloudless sky, as a light breeze from the northward filled the sails of a small yacht which glided smoothly along the southern coast of England. At the helm of the little vessel stood her owner, Captain Maynard, a retired naval officer. Next to his fair young daughter, Clara, the old sailor looked upon his yacht as one of the most beautiful things in existence. Though her crew consisted but of two men and a boy, and she measured scarcely five-and-twenty tons, he declared that if it were necessary he would sail round the world in her without the slightest hesitation.

" Flatten in the jib, and take a pull at the main-sheet, my lads, and we shall run into the bay without a tack, if the wind holds as it does now," he sang out.

The men, as they came aft to execute the latter order, had to disturb some of the passengers, of whom there were several, seated on cloaks round the sky-light, or standing up holding on to the weather rigging, or leaning against the main-boom. Clara Maynard, accustomed to yachting, promptly moved to windward, aided by Harry Caulfield, a young military officer, who had ridden over that morning to Luton, for the pleasure of making a trip on board the yacht; but her aunt, Miss Sarah Pemberton, looked somewhat annoyed at being asked to shift her seat. Harry, however, came to her assistance, and placed a camp-stool for her against the weather bulwarks.

"I am sorry, Sarah, to inconvenience you," said the captain, good-naturedly, "but we haven't as much room on board the *Ariadne* as on the deck of a line-of-battle ship."

The captain had called his yacht after the first ship in which he went to sea.

The cutter having rounded a lofty point, a small and beautiful bay opened out ahead; and the wind remaining steady, without making another tack, she stood in directly for it.

"We could not have chosen a more lovely spot for our picnic," exclaimed

Clara. " See, Aunt Sarah—I am sure you will be pleased when you get there. Watch those picturesque cliffs, ever changing in shape as we sail along—and see those breezy downs above them, and the fine yellow sands below, and that pretty valley with the old fisherman's cottage on one side, and the clear stream running down its centre, and leaping over the rocks in a tiny cascade."

" I shall be very glad to get safe on shore," answered Miss Pemberton, who had been persuaded, much against her will, to venture for the first time on board the little *Ariadne.*

She had been invited, on the death of Clara's mother, her younger sister, to take up her abode with her widowed brother-in-law, and had only lately accepted his frequently repeated offer. Whatever good qualities she might have possessed, she was certainly not attractive in appearance, being tall and thin, with a cold and forbidding manner. Clara treated her aunt with due respect, and did all she could to win her affections, though she tried in vain to bestow that love she would willingly have given. Miss Pemberton presented a strong contrast to her niece, who was generally admired. Clara was very fair, of moderate height, and of a slight and elegant figure, with regular features and a pleasing smile ; though a physiognomist might have suspected that she wanted the valuable quality of firmness, which in her position was especially necessary ; for she already possessed a good fortune, and would inherit a considerable one. Her father, although a sailor of the old school, was not destitute of discernment, and thoroughly understanding her character, earnestly wished to see her married to a sensible, upright man, who would protect her and take good care of her property. He had therefore given every encouragement to Harry Caulfield, son of his old and esteemed friend, General Caulfield. He had known and liked Harry from his boyhood, and fully believed that he possessed those sterling qualities which would tend to secure' his daughter's happiness. Harry had met her when staying with some friends at Cheltenham, and admired her before he knew that she possessed a fortune. He had thus the satisfaction of feeling that his love was purely disinterested. Of this she was aware, and it had greatly influenced her in returning his affection. When Clara wrote to her father, from whom she had no concealments, to tell him of the attention she was receiving from Captain Caulfield, his reply was, "I am very glad indeed to hear it ; nothing could give me greater pleasure. Tell him to come down to Luton, and that I shall be delighted to see him."

Clara shortly afterwards returned home with her Aunt Sarah, and Harry of course followed, accompanied by his father, the general, who, finding a house in the neighbourhood vacant, engaged it for the sake of being near Captain Maynard, and thus enabling the young people to be together without depriving himself of his son's society. Harry's regiment was in India, and he was under orders to rejoin it. Though fond of his profession, in which he had gained distinction, and had every prospect of rising, he at first thought of selling out; but to this his father objected, and even Captain Maynard agreed that, as Clara was very young, they might wait a couple of years till he

had obtained another step in rank, and
that he would then consent to her accompanying him back, if necessary, to India.
The course of true love in this instance
appeared to run smoothly enough.   Harry
was most devoted in his attentions, and
admired Clara more and more every day
he spent with her—while she was satisfied
that it would be impossible for her to
love any one more ; and had not she felt
that it was her duty to remain with her
father, she would willingly have married
at once, and gone out to India.   She saw
clearly, however, that her Aunt Sarah was
not suited to take her place or attend to
her father, as she had observed of late
that his health was failing, so that even
for Harry's sake she could not bring
herself to quit him.   She had therefore
consented to Harry's leaving her, though
not without a severe struggle.   It was the

first shadow which had come over her young and hitherto happy life since the loss of her beloved mother. She was convinced that Harry was in every way worthy of her affections. He was a fine, handsome fellow, with frank agreeable manners, and a large amount of good sense and judgment. He had managed even to win the good opinion of Miss Sarah Pemberton, who was not in general inclined to think well of young men especially of officers in the army, whom she designated generally as an impudent, profligate set, with fluent tongues and insinuating manners, whose chief occupation in life was to break the hearts of young girls foolish enough to trust them.

Among the rest of the company on board the yacht was Mary Lennard, a girl of about fourteen years old, a sweet young creature, and a great favourite of

Clara's. She was the daughter of the Reverend John Lennard, who had been for some years vicar of the parish of Luton-cum-Crosham, but only as *locum tenens*, he having been requested to take charge of it by the patron, Sir Richard Bygrave, who had promised to bestow it on his young relative, Dick Rushworth, as soon as Dick was of an age to take orders. The said Dick Rushworth, however, having lately unexpectedly come into a fortune, had quitted the university, and declined becoming a clergyman; and Sir Reginald, influenced by his wife, had bestowed the living on her cousin, the Reverend Ambrose Lerew, who had graduated at Oxford, and had been for some time a curate in that diocese. He had lately married a lady somewhat older than himself, possessed of a fair fortune, who had been considered a belle during two or three

London seasons, but had failed to secure such a matrimonial alliance as she and her friends considered that she ought to make when she first came out. At length, awakening to the fact that her youth was passing away and her beauty fading, she had consented to give her hand, and as much of a heart as she possessed, to the fashionable-looking and well-connected young curate, an especial favourite of her friend, Lady Bygrave.

Mr. Lennard had held the living longer than he had expected, and to the best of his ability had done his duty to his parishioners. He was a genial, warm-hearted man, of good presence; his manners urbane and courteous; fond of a joke, hospitable and kind, being consequently a favourite with all classes. The more wealthy liked him for his pleasant conversation and readiness to

enter into all their gaieties and amuse-
ments, and the poorer for the kind way
in which he spoke to them, and the
assistance he afforded on all occasions
when they were in distress. He had
lost his wife two or three years after
he became vicar of Luton-cum-Crosham.
She had left two children, his dear little
Mary, and a son, Alfred, a tall, pale-faced
youth, who was now on board the yacht.
The young gentleman had been with a
tutor, and was about to go up to Oxford.
He was considered very well-behaved; but
as he seldom gave expression to his
opinions, no one could ascertain much
about his character, or how he was likely
to turn out. His father always spoke
of him as his good boy, who had never
given him any trouble, and he fully
believed never would cause him a moment's anxiety. His tutor had sent him

home with a high character for diligence in his studies, and attention to his religious duties, which consisted in a regular attendance at church and at the morning and evening prayers of the family; and his father was happy in the belief that he would do very well in the world as a clergyman, or at the bar, or in any other profession he might select. Still, Mary was undoubtedly his favourite, and on her he bestowed the full affection of a father's heart. She was indeed a most loveable little creature. Clara was especially fond of her. Mary was so clever and sensible, that she was always a welcome guest at Luton.

Besides the persons already mentioned on board the yacht, there was Lieutenant Sims, of the coastguard, with his wife and daughter; a Mrs. and Miss Prentiss, the latter young and pretty; Tom Wesby, a friend of Alfred Lennard's, very like him

in appearance and manner; and an artist
engaged in sketching in the neighbourhood, who had brought a letter of introduction to Captain Maynard.

As the cutter rounded the headland
before spoken of, most of the party
evinced their admiration of the scenery
by expressions of delight, and the artist
exhibited his skill by making a faithful
sketch in a few minutes. The wind
freshening, the cutter made rapid progress
towards the bay. Harry had taken the
telescope, and was directing it towards
the shore.

" Some of our party are there already,"
he exclaimed ; " I see my father and Mr.
Lennard, and I conclude that the other
people must be the new vicar and his
wife, from the unmistakable cut of the
gentleman's coat, and the lady's irre-
proachable costume. There are several

nore, though I cannot exactly make out who they are; I see, however, that the servants are bringing down the baskets of provisions, so we need have no fear of starving."

"I did not expect that they would arrive so soon. The wind has been light, and we have had the tide against us," observed Captain Maynard. "It will run long enough, however, to take us home again, if you young people are on board in good time. I must trust to you, Harry, to collect all our passengers; or, should the wind drop, we may find ourselves drifting down Channel for the best part of the night."

"Oh! that will be capital fun," cried Mrs. Sims. "Mary, you'd like it amazingly. We can sit on deck, and look at the stars, and sing songs, and have our tea, and listen to the sailors' yarns———"

"And have the chance of being run down and sunk by one of those big blundering iron steam-kettles," growled the lieutenant, who had the antipathy long felt by old sailors to all the modern innovations, as he considered them, in the navy.

As the cutter glided up towards the shore, the party standing on the beach waved their handkerchiefs, and the ladies on board waved theirs. The jib was taken in, the foresail hauled down, and the yacht rounding to, the anchor was let drop at a short distance from the beach.

"Haul the boat up alongside, Tom," said Captain Maynard. "Now, Mr. Sims, I must get you to take charge of the first party for the shore."

"With the greatest pleasure in the world; I am always at the service of the ladies," answered the lieutenant, bowing round to them, "but my difficulty is to know who is to go first, unless I select by seniority. Miss Sarah Pemberton, suppose I ask you—age before honesty, you know."

"You do not wish to insult me, Mr. Sims?" answered the lady, bridling up.

"Come, come, Sally, Sims never thought of such a thing; he was only joking, or rather, let the words slip out of his mouth without knowing what he was saying," said Captain Maynard.

"I am not fond of joking," replied Miss Sarah; "but if you wish me to go first, I shall be very glad to get on shore, I assure you."

"Pardon me, madam," said the lieutenant, looking very penitent, and offering his hand. "I wouldn't say a word to ruffle your sensitive feelings, I do assure you."

Miss Pemberton, being appeased, gave

her hand to the lieutenant, and though she at first showed some signs of trepidation, stepped without difficulty into the stern-sheets of the boat. She was followed by Mrs. and Miss Sims.

"Come, young Lennard, you get into the bows, and help to trim the boat," said Mr. Sims; and shoving off, they pulled for the shore.

The boat soon reached the beach, when Mr. Alfred, jumping out, wetted his shoes, greatly to his annoyance, and went running off without stopping to offer his assistance to the ladies. Some of the rest of the party, however, came down to welcome them, and Mrs. and Miss Sims, being accustomed to boating, having jumped out, the lieutenant was able to aid Miss Pemberton in performing that, to her, hazardous operation.

"Trust to me, my good lady," he said

in an encouraging tone; "now step on this thwart—now on the next—now on the gunwale."

"What's that?" asked Miss Pemberton.

"The side of the boat, I should have said," answered the lieutenant. "Now spring with all the agility you possess." At which the lady gave a bound which nearly overset the gallant officer, and would have ended by bringing her down on the sand, had not General Caulfield caught her in his arms.

"I hope you are not hurt, my dear madam!" he exclaimed.

"I have nearly dislocated my ancle, I believe," answered Miss Pemberton. "It is the first time I have ventured on board a yacht, and I intend that it shall be the last, with my own good pleasure."

On this the Reverend Mr. Lerew

stepped forward and expressed his sympathy to Miss Pemberton, offering her his arm to conduct her up to a rock under the cliff, where she could sit and rest her injured foot.

"I feel grieved for you, my dear madam, that what was intended to be a party of pleasure should commence with so untoward an event," he said. "Do allow my wife to examine your injured ancle—she is all tenderness and sympathy, and a gentle rubbing may perhaps restore it to its wonted elasticity."

"I hope that I shall recover after a little rest, without giving Mrs. Lerew the trouble," answered Miss Pemberton, touched with the interest exhibited by the new vicar. "I am deeply grateful to you. But those sea-officers, though well-intentioned, including my poor dear brother-in-law, are dreadfully rough and unmannerly, and have not ceased to alarm and annoy me since I got on board that horrible little vessel, misnamed a pleasure yacht."

"True charity would make me wish to gloss over their faults—though I must confess I agree with you, my dear lady; but we must consider it the result of their early education, or rather, want of education," observed Mr. Lerew, in a soft voice; "I fear, too, that their religious training is as defective as their manners—we must, however, use our best endeavours to correct the former, though it may be hopeless to attempt an improvement in the latter—indeed, it is of so infinitely less consequence, that provided we are successful in imparting the true faith, we must rest satisfied."

"Oh, yes, I daresay I do," answered Miss Pemberton, who was thinking more about her ancle than of what Mr. Lerew was saying to her; catching one of his words, she added, "but I don't accuse my brother-in-law of being irreligious; I assure you, he reads prayers every morning as the clock strikes half-past eight, and every evening at ten, with a chapter from the Old and New Testaments, with Ryle's expositions."

"Pray, what prayers does he use?" asked Mr. Lerew, in a tone which showed that he considered the matter of great importance.

"He generally uses Bickersteth's prayers," answered Miss Pemberton.

"Sad! sad!" exclaimed Mr. Lerew, in a tone of horror, "thus to neglect the Prayer-Book and submit to the teaching of men the most deadly enemies of the catholic faith. Do let me entreat you to beg that he will banish Ryle and Bickersteth from his library, or rather, commit them—I should say their works—to the flames at once, lest they should fall into the hands of *other ignorant* people."

"I never thought there was any harm in them," answered Miss Pemberton, somewhat astonished at the vehemence with which the new vicar condemned his two brother divines, whom she had hitherto considered sound, trustworthy teachers. "I will mention what you say to my brother-in-law, but I suspect that he will not be easily induced to do as you advise. I know that he considers Canon Ryle a very sensible and pious man, and I have often heard him say that he could understand his writings better than those of any one else he ever met with."

"Blind leaders of the blind," said Mr. Lerew. "The pernicious principles of such men are calculated to produce the overthrow of our Holy Church, and to under-mine all catholic doctrines."

"Dear me, Mr. Lerew, I always thought Ryle and Bickersteth very sound church-men and firm advocates of the truth," said Miss Pemberton.

"Alas! alas! my dear lady; I fear there are many wolves in sheep's clothing who have long beguiled their flocks by teaching them to rely on their own judg-ment, instead of seeking for counsel and advice from those pastors who, knowing themselves to be duly appointed from on high to administer the holy sacraments, and grant absolution to humble penitents, feel the importance of their sacred office," replied Mr. Lerew.

Miss Pemberton did not quite under-stand Mr. Lerew's meaning; but as he exhibited so much feeling and sympathy for her sprained ancle, she sat and listened, and thought that, though he was less agreeable than Mr. Lennard, he at all events must be a very pious and excellent young clergyman, and that since the vicar, who had been so generally liked, was compelled to resign his office, it was fortunate for the parishioners that they had obtained so *superior* a *minister*.

In the meantime the boat had returned to the yacht for another freight, Captain Maynard, with Harry, Clara, and Mary, being the last to land. By this time most of the party had collected on the beach to welcome them. General Caulfield, after shaking hands with the captain, led off Clara, for the sake, as he said, of having a little talk with her. He was very fond of his future daughter-in-law, who was exactly the girl he desired as a wife for his son. While they were absent, the captain chose a shady spot under the cliff for spreading the table-cloth. The younger members of the party, under the superintendence of Mrs. Sims, were busily engaged in unpacking the hampers and baskets, and arranging their contents.

"Alfred, ahoy! bear a hand, and place the knives and forks alongside the plates; I like to see young men making themselves useful, instead of throwing all the work upon the ladies," exclaimed Captain Maynard, as he saw young Lennard sauntering off by himself, to avoid the trouble of speaking to any one. Thus summoned, Alfred was compelled to return, when Mary, with a merry laugh, put a bundle of knives and forks into his hands, and told him to go and arrange some on the opposite side of the cloth. The picnic had been got up by some of the principal people in the parish, as a compliment to their former vicar, as also for the purpose of enabling his successor to become acquainted with them in an easy and pleasant way. Sir Reginald and Lady Bygrave had been invited, but had not yet arrived, and it would, of course, have been uncourteous to commence luncheon, hungry as everybody was, till they appeared. The party had, in the meantime, to amuse themselves according to their tastes; some of the ladies had brought their sketch-books, others their work—though the greater number preferred doing nothing.

The ever busy Lieutenant Sims had sent off to the yacht for an iron pot, which he filled up with potatoes and salt water, and having called some of the young gentlemen to assist him in collecting a quantity of dry wood which was seen scattered along the beach, he made a

large fire, and put on the pot to boil.
"Now, by boys, take a lesson from an
old tar," he observed. "Whenever you
want to cook potatoes to perfection, boil
them in salt water if you can get it, or if
not, put in plenty of salt, and let them
remain till the water has evaporated.
You will then have them come out like
lumps of meal, as these will, you'll see,
before long."

Harry had soon stolen off, and joined
Clara and his father. The latter shortly
after left the young people to themselves,
while he went back to meet Captain
Maynard and Mr. Lennard, who were
strolling along the beach.

"I feel perfectly satisfied with my successor, as far as I am able at present to
judge," observed Mr. Lennard. "He is a
wonderfully zealous and earnest man. He
shows an evident desire to make himself

popular, and to win the affections of the people ; and I cannot blame him if he seems surprised that I have not introduced some of the more modern improvements in churches."

"For my part, I hope that what he calls improvements will not follow the direction of the changes which have been made in some parishes," observed General Caulfield. "There are many who would object to them, as I should myself, and they can produce no real good."

"New brooms sweep clean," said Mr. Lennard. "He naturally wishes to be doing something, and I shall not be jealous. It is all-important to have peace and good-will in the parish."

"It may be bought at too dear a price," said General Caulfield, "but we will hope for the best. Here comes Mrs. Lerew ; she was, I understand, a good deal in

London society, and is an elegant and fashionable-looking person, though she is somewhat older than Lerew, I suspect."

"She may not make the worse wife for that," observed Captain Maynard.

Harry and Clara had wandered away from the rest of the party, and were seated on a rock, at some distance off. She had brought her sketch-book, and was endeavouring to make a drawing of the bay, with the headland to the eastward, round which they had come, and the little yacht at anchor off the beach ; but anxious as she was to produce a satisfactory sketch, a duplicate of which Harry had begged her to give to him, her hand trembled, and her heart felt very sad. It was the last day they were to be together, and she thought of the long, long months which must elapse before he was to return.

"My memory will often fly back to this

spot when I am far away," said Harry; "and though leagues of land and ocean divide us, we shall here meet in spirit and talk to each other, shall we not, dearest?"

"I am sure of it," said Clara, looking into his handsome, honest countenance. "I wish that I could make a better sketch, but I will try to improve it at home."

"Oh! no, no! leave it just as it is; I wish to think of you as you are now," said Harry, "my own dear girl; and I would rather see every line as you have traced it on the paper before my eyes."

"Well, then, I will keep the copy for myself," said Clara; "or I can come here with papa in the yacht, and take it over again."

The sketch was finished, and seeing their friends assembling, and Mrs. Sims beckoning vehemently to them, they rose to return.

"I hope that my father will remain at Updown till I come back," said Harry. "You will always trust to him, Clara, as to one who loves you as his daughter; and it will be a happiness to me to know that he will be near you, should Captain Maynard's health fail."

Clara sighed. "I much fear that is likely to happen—indeed, I have been unable to conceal from myself that he has greatly altered lately."

Harry, wishing to avoid melancholy thoughts, changed the subject.

"I am not quite satisfied with your new vicar," he observed; "I am afraid that he belongs to a school of which I have the utmost possible dread. Believe me, dearest, I was most thankful to find, when I first came down to Luton, that Captain Maynard held the opinions I do, and that your parish was free from any of the ritualistic practices of the day. Much as all must like Mr. Lennard for his pleasant manners and kind heart, he is not exactly what I should wish a clergyman to be, but he is at all events thoroughly sound in practice. Believe me, Clara, that however much I might admire a girl, and be inclined to love her, I would not risk my domestic happiness by marrying, should I find that she was enslaved by those plotting the overthrow of the Protestant principles of our Church. You know, dearest, how strongly I feel on the subject, and I trust that you will, for your own sake, as well as mine, withstand all the allurements and artifices which either lay or clerical ritualists. may use to induce you to support or take a part in their practices."

"I hope so," said Clara, "though Lady

Bygrave, when last she called on us, told me that there are many true and devoted men who are called ritualists; and I cannot say that I see any objection to good music and elegantly built churches, which it is their chief aim to introduce for the purpose of forwarding the cause of religion and devotion. Many people are dissatisfied with the untrained attempts at harmony in our too often unsightly churches."

Harry was going to reply, but he found that the last remark had been made unintentionally in the hearing of Mr. Lerew. That gentleman watched his opportunity, and while Harry had left Clara's side for a moment, he observed in a low, soft voice, " I see, Miss Maynard, that you are a young lady of good taste, and above the vulgar prejudices of the Calvinistic school, who stubbornly refuse to dedicate the best of their substance and talents to God, and rest satisfied with offering to Him the ugliest buildings their imaginations can devise, and the refuse of their possessions."

He stopped on seeing Harry, who quickly rejoined Clara.

"Here they come! here they come!" exclaimed several of the most hungry of the party, as a tall gentleman and lady, accompanied by two sombre, well-dressed persons, were seen descending the hill

"Who can those people be with Sir Reginald and Lady Bygrave, I wonder?' cried Mrs. Sims; "they look to me for all the world like Jesuit priests."

Mr. Lerew's countenance brightened, and Master Alfred Lennard showed more interest than he had hitherto exhibited in any of the proceedings of the day.

"So I fear they are," observed General Caulfield. "What can have induced Sir Reginald and his wife to bring them here?"

Mr. Lerew, however, with several other persons, hurried up the pathway, to greet the chief people of that part of their county. Lady Bygrave, escorted by one of the priests, who gave her his hand at the steeper parts of the path, came first, and at once introduced their friend Monsieur l'Abbé Hénon, who with his companion, Father Lascelles, had arrived only that morning, and had begged leave to accompany them. They had come to see Sir Reginald on the subject of forming a new settlement in South America, as it was well known he was deeply interested in the subject of colonisation, and they hoped to obtain his influence and support.

"They are most delightful people,"

whispered Lady Bygrave to Miss Pemberton, who met her ladyship at the bottom of the descent ; " everybody will be pleased with them, they are so full of information, and so free from prejudices —they will disabuse all our minds of the vulgar notion that Catholic priests can talk of nothing but masses and penances ; and they are so noble-minded and philanthropic.

The abbé, who overheard what was said, smiled blandly, and addressed himself to Miss Pemberton. He spoke English perfectly, with only a slight foreign accent, in a melodious voice, attractive and soothing to his hearers. He and Father Lascelles bowed politely as they were introduced to the company, and at once made themselves at home, uttering not a word to which even the most prejudiced could object.

Lady Bygrave was still young, with a decidedly aristocratic appearance, and very pleasant manners when she had to be condescending. Sir Reginald was a tall, good-looking man, who seldom expressed an opinion, his florid countenance not exhibiting any large amount of intellect; but as he was considered straightforward and honest, he was generally liked.

With as little delay as possible, not to show the last comers too much that they had been waited for, the party assembled round the ample repast; and while the older gentlemen were employed in carving, the younger ones, aided by Mrs. Sims, busied themselves in carrying round the plates. The usual conversation at picnics then became general. The abbé and his companion, having glanced round the company, and carefully noted each person present, were soon enabled to take part in it. They said nothing very remarkable, but managed, notwithstanding, to draw out the opinions of most of those to whom they addressed themselves. The abbé was especially attentive to Mr. and Mrs. Lerew, and both seemed highly flattered with what he said. He fixed his glance on Master Alfred, and having ascertained who he was, spoke to him in a gentle, encouraging tone. Mr. Lennard himself seemed pleased with Sir Reginald's visitors, and remarked to General Caulfield that he had seldom met more agreeable foreigners.

"I don't trust them," answered the general; "the more pleasant and insinuating they are, the more necessary it is to avoid them. I would never allow such men to enter my house or become intimate with any of my family."

Captain Maynard entertained much the same feeling as his friend. Lieutenant Sims never did care about foreigners, and thought the idea of getting Englishmen to emigrate to such a country as they talked of was all humbug. The abbé and his friends might have heard many of the observations made; but whether complimentary or not, they did not allow a muscle of their countenances to change. Lady Bygrave happened to upset her wineglass, and soon afterwards the abbé did exactly the same thing; on which he turned with a bow to her ladyship, observing, " I am sure whatever Lady Bygrave does is the right thing, and cannot therefore be reproved."

" I am thankful, Monsieur l'Abbé," said Lady Bygrave, smiling. " I am sure that I can always rely upon you for support."

"Ah, yes, madam, in spiritual matters as in temporal," whispered the abbé.

The conversation was, however, generally of a lively character, and all agreed that the picnic was a success, and that they had enjoyed themselves amazingly. Captain Maynard, however, looking at his watch, declared that those who intended to return in the yacht must come on board without delay. Miss Pemberton declined, if she could possibly get a conveyance, and Lady Bygrave offered to take her in her carriage; Father Lascelles begging leave to return in a pony-carriage which had brought the hampers, if some one who knew the way would drive him — on which Alfred Lennard requested to be allowed the honour of doing so. Harry and Clara of course went back in the yacht, as did the rest of the party who had come in her.

"Mr. Lennard must take care that that Jesuit priest does not get hold of his son," observed Harry to Clara; "you might get Mary to speak to her father and warn him, for he seemed as much pleased with the strangers as Sir Reginald and Lady Bygrave. I hold with my father about them; and I would as soon trust a couple of serpents within my doors."

"Are you not rather severe on the poor men?" asked Clara.

"Knowing their principles and their great object—to bring under subjection the minds of their fellow-creatures, and thus to amass wealth for the purpose of raising their order above all the ruling powers on earth—I cannot say anything too severe. To attain their ends they will allow nothing to stand in their way; they will hesitate at no crime, no deceit;

they will assume any character which suits them, and will undertake the lowest offices, and will employ the vilest means, or will pretend to the most exalted piety."

"Surely, Harry, the men we saw to-day could not be guilty of such conduct," said Clara.

"Every Jesuit is trained in the same school, and I therefore make no exceptions," answered Harry. "We shall find that even those gentlemen, fascinating as they appeared, had some object in visiting Sir Reginald, ulterior to that of presenting him with a scheme of colonisation. He is wealthy; and depend on it, they were informed of the proclivities of Lady Bygrave."

Clara was not quite convinced. It was not likely, however, that the abbé and his companion would pay a visit to Luton.

Chapter II.

HARRY had gone. Clara felt very sad; her eye was constantly at the telescope in the drawing-room, looking out for the steamer which was conveying him to Alexandria. She at length caught sight of a long white line and a puff ot grey smoke above it, which she believed must belong to the ship. She was still watching it as it was growing less and less distinct, when her aunt, entering the room, said, " I am afraid that your father is very ill. I went into his study just now; when I spoke to him, he was unable to answer me."

Clara flew to the study, and found her father seated in his arm-chair. There was a pained expression in his eyes, and he was speechless. He had been seized with a paralytic stroke. The servant was immediately despatched to bring the doctor, who was found not far off, and quickly came. He pronounced the captain to be in considerable danger. Clara, ever dutiful and affectionate, was constant in her attendance on her father. Even Miss Pemberton's manner softened, and she did her best to comfort her niece. In the course of two or three days, Captain Maynard had somewhat recovered, and was able to speak without much difficulty. General Caulfield, who had heard of his illness, came over to see him. The brave sailor believed himself to be dying.

" It is a knock at my door to which I am bound to attend, General," he said.

"I have no fear for myself, for I trust in One 'mighty to save;' but I am anxious about my gentle Clara, so ill able to battle with the troubles of life. I wish that we had not let Harry go; I could have left her with confidence in his care. Would that he could be recalled!"

"His ship is across the bay by this time. We acted for the best, and must trust to Him who ever cares for the orphan and widow. While I live, I will be a father to your child, and assist her aunt in watching over her," answered the general; "but cheer up, my friend, I do not speak to one ignorant of the truth, and therefore I can say that God may still preserve your life for her sake, though you will undoubtedly be the gainer by going hence, as all are who die in the Lord. We can pray to Him to protect her." And the gallant old soldier knelt down by the side of his friend, as by that of a beloved brother, and together they lifted up their voices to Him in whom they trusted. Though Captain Maynard could but faintly repeat the words uttered by the general, his heart spoke with the fervency of a true Christian who expects soon to be in the presence of his Saviour. He pressed the general's hand. "And whatever happens, my dear friend, I feel confident that you will fulfil your promise," he said.

Before the general left the house, he spoke for some time to Miss Pemberton, who was fully convinced that her brother-in-law had not many hours to live. The captain, however, the next day had greatly recovered; and while Miss Pemberton was seated in the drawing-room, Clara being with her father, Mr. and Mrs. Lerew were announced. Mrs. Lerew advancing, took Miss Pemberton's hand, and sank into a seat, her husband following with the most obsequious of bows and blandest of smiles.

"My dear lady, I rejoice to find you within," he said, "as I am anxious to have some earnest conversation with you, while perhaps, if I may venture to make the request, your niece will show the garden to Mrs. Lerew."

"Clara is with her father, who is still, I regret to say, very ill," answered Miss Pemberton ; "but I will summon her, that she may have the pleasure of seeing Mrs. Lerew."

"Not for the world," answered the vicar : "the present opportunity is propitious. I was aware of Captain Maynard's serious illness; indeed, I am most desirous to speak to him on the subject of his soul's welfare. From what his medical attendant tells me, I fear that his days are numbered ; and you will pardon me when I say it, I grieve to hear that he has been sadly neglectful of his religious duties."

"I hope you are mistaken," answered Miss Pemberton, somewhat astonished at the remark ; "though I have not resided long with him, I have always understood that he was specially attentive to them."

"Not to some of the most important," said Mr. Lerew : "he has not once been to the celebration of the Holy Eucharist since I became vicar of the parish, nor has he attended matin-song or even-song, which I have performed daily ; and I regret to observe that neither you nor your niece have been present."

"My brother-in-law has not been in the habit of attending any but Sunday services, nor have I, I confess," said Miss

Pemberton; "but I shall be very happy, if he gets better, to drive over with my niece, should you think it right."

"Right!" exclaimed Mr. Lerew in a tone of amazement; "I consider it a great sin to neglect such means of grace, and by neglecting them you encourage others to do so likewise; whereas if people of position set a good example, it will be followed by their inferiors. But, my dear lady, I fear that I have said what may sound harsh in your ears. One of my great objects to-day is to see your brother-in-law alone, and I must ask you to enable me to do so while Mrs. Lerew is paying her respects to your niece."

Miss Pemberton, seeing no objection to this, undertook to send Clara down, and to beg Captain Maynard to receive the vicar. She went upstairs for this purpose. Of course the sick man could not decline the vicar's visit, and Clara having very unwillingly left her father, Mr. Lerew was ushered into his room. The new vicar spoke softly and gently, and expressed his sorrow to hear of the captain's serious illness. He then went on to speak of the importance of being prepared for death.

"I would urge you, therefore, my dear sir, to confess your sins to me, that I may absolve you from them, as I have authority from my office."

"Yes, sir, I have many sins to confess, and I have already with hearty repentance done so to my God," answered the captain, sitting up in bed. "I am very sure, too, that they are all washed away in the blood of Jesus Christ."

The vicar gave a suppressed hem. He at once saw that he must drop the point of confession. "Then, my dear

sir," he added, " I should have no hesitation in administering to you the Holy
Eucharist, which, knowing your dangerous
state, I reserved for you on Sunday last,
and have now brought in my pocket."

" I do not exactly understand you, sir,"
answered the captain, wondering what his
visitor could mean.

"You would surely wish to enjoy the
benefit of that Holy Sacrament," said the
vicar, " and I have brought the conse-
crated elements with me, the wafer and
the wine mingled with water, which latter
it is lawful in the Anglican Church to
administer."

" I understand you now, and am much
obliged to you for your kind intentions,"
said the captain " but the truth is, I
should prefer taking the sacrament with
my old friends, Mr. Lennard and General
Caulfield, with my daughter, and sister-in-

law, and the members of my household. We have always an ample supply
of bread and wine for the purpose."

"Of my predecessor I say nothing, and
hope that he will be brought ere long
to the knowledge and practice of the
truth," exclaimed Mr. Lerew. "General
Caulfield—pardon me for saying it—is, I
understand, a schismatic with whom we
are bound to hold no communion. He
has for several Sundays attended a
dissenting conventicle, and actually takes
upon himself to preach and to attempt
to teach his ignorant fellow-creatures;
for ignorant and benighted those must
be who listen to him. It will be at
the peril of your soul, I am bound to
tell you, Captain Maynard, should you
invite him to be present at the awful
ceremony you propose to hold."

"I will be responsible for the risk I

may run," answered Captain Maynard, the spirit of the old sailor rising within him. " I cannot allow my dearest friend, in whose truly religious character I have unbounded confidence, to be so spoken of without protest. In my state, especially, I would quarrel with no man. You made a mistake, Mr. Lerew, in thus speaking of that excellent man."

" I deeply regret it," said the vicar. " I must not longer intrude on you, but I am bound to tell you, Captain Maynard, that I consider your soul in imminent danger, and I earnestly pray that another day, ere it be too late, a benign influence may induce you more willingly to receive my ministrations. Farewell." And Mr. Lerew, rising with a frowning brow, walked to the door, while the captain, sinking back on his pillow, rang his bell. Soon after Mr.

Lerew had returned to the drawing-room, the servant entered to say that the captain wished to see Miss Clara, and she, without even stopping to say good-bye to her guests, hurried upstairs.

The vicar's manner was calm as usual. Miss Pemberton had scarcely time to ask whether he had had a satisfactory inter-view with her brother-in-law, when Lieutenant and Mrs. Sims entered the room. Miss Pemberton was compelled to shake hands with them, as the lieutenant advanced in his usual hearty fashion, but she showed that their arrival caused her no great satisfaction. Mr. Lerew and his wife received them in a stiff manner, and the former held out two fingers, which Sims nearly dislocated as he grasped them in his rough palm. The lieutenant, having enquired after Captain Maynard, and being informed by Miss Pemberton that he was as well as she could hope, found himself compelled to relapse into silence, as Mr. Lerew, giving a hint to his wife to attend to Mrs. Sims, requested a few moments' conversation with Miss Pemberton in the bay window. Leading the lady to it, he spoke in so low a voice, that even Mrs. Sims, much as she might have wished to do so, could not catch a word—while the honest lieutenant, who did not trouble himself about the matter, endeavoured to make amends for the somewhat unintelligible replies which his wife gave to Mrs. Lerew.

The first portion of the vicar's conversation had reference to Clara; he then continued in the same suppressed tone, "The General, also, is not a man on whose religious opinions you should place reliance, my dear madam, and I would especially urge you to prevent him, by every means in your power, from coming here. He can only lead your poor brother-in-law from the right path, and may induce him to refrain from taking advantage of the sacred offices I am so anxious to render."

In a few minutes Mr. Lerew and Miss Pemberton returned to their seats, the former observing in a voice which he intended should be heard, "General Caulfield may be a very worthy soldier, but I unhesitatingly say, and I wish it to be known, that I consider any person, whatever his rank, is to be greatly blamed who enters a dissenting chapel, and without authority pretends to preach to the ignorant populace."

"But, sir, I can say I once listened to as good a sermon preached by the general as I ever heard from parson or bishop, begging your pardon," exclaimed Mr. Sims, the colour mounting to his honest cheeks as he spoke ; " he preaches simply from the Bible, and just says what the Bible says·; and that, I hold, is the best test of a good sermon."

" The Bible, Mr. Sims, is a very dangerous book, if read by the laity, without the proper interpretation of those deputed by Holy Church to explain its meaning," emphatically replied Mr. Lerew.

The lieutenant gave an involuntary whew. " Then I suppose that you mean the Bible should not be read by us laity," he exclaimed.

" Certainly, not without the written or verbal explanation of the priests of our Church," answered Mr. Lerew.

" And that is your opinion ? " asked the lieutenant, resolving then and there that he would never allow the vicar an opportunity of explaining the Bible to him or any of his family according to his interpretation ; " and you wish this to be known in the parish, Mr. Lerew ? "

" Certainly, I do not desire to conceal my opinions—I speak with authority," answered the vicar.

" But, my dear, the people may misunderstand you," observed Mrs. Lerew, who reflected that her husband had made an acknowledgment which some of his parishioners might take up, and perhaps cause him annoyance ; but the vicar was not a man to be withheld from expressing his opinion by any such fears. He was aware that he would be supported by Sir Reginald and Lady Bygrave, and he secretly held such persons as Lieutenant Sims and the rest of his parishioners of inferior rank in the utmost contempt.

"I will take good care that your opinion is known, though I do not agree with it, I can tell you, Mr. Lerew," exclaimed the lieutenant, rising. "I am sorry, Miss Pemberton, that I cannot see my excellent friend this morning. I served under him six years or more—there is no man I more esteem, and I know what his opinion is of General Caulfield. Give him my love and respects, and say I hope to have a talk with him another day when he is better. Come, my dear, it is time we should be jogging home."

This was said to his wife; and the two rising, took their departure, receiving the most freezing of looks from the vicar and the two ladies. At that instant a servant girl entered, to beg that Miss Pemberton would come up immediately into her master's room.

"We didn't like to interrupt you, marm, but I am afraid the captain's in a bad way," she said,

"I will attend you," exclaimed Mr. Lerew: "a priest is ever in his proper place beside the bed of the dying."

Without waiting for permission, he followed Miss Pemberton into Captain Maynard's room. Clara was at her father's bedside, holding his hand. She had found him, when she returned from the drawing-room after his interview with the vicar, speechless. He had endeavoured to say something to her, but his tongue refused its office; his mind was, however, it was evident, unimpaired. He looked up with a pained expression, and tried to show that he wished to write; but when a slate was brought him, his fingers were unable to hold the pencil. Clara had immediately sent off for the doctor, and was now endeavouring, by chafing her father's hands, to restore their power.

On seeing the vicar in the doorway, a peculiar expression passed over Captain Maynard's countenance, and he made another desperate effort to utter a few words in his daughter's ear, but in vain— no articulate sounds proceeded from his lips.

"I feel the deepest sympathy and compassion for you, my dear young lady," said the vicar in a gentle tone. "We will pray for the soul of the departing—join me, I beseech you— induce your niece to kneel with us," he whispered to Miss Pemberton, who nodded, and placing a chair by the bedside, almost compelled Clara to kneel on it, while she continued the act of filial affection in which she had been engaged. The vicar then taking from his pocket a book, read a service, of which poor Clara, agitated as she was, did not comprehend a word. Captain Maynard all the time was looking into her fair face with the same pained expression in his eyes which they had assumed on the entrance of the vicar. Doctor Brown, a worthy and excellent man, arrived just as the vicar had concluded; and exercising his authority, requested him and Miss Pemberton to leave the room, observing that perfect quiet was necessary for his patient.

"You may stay," he whispered to Miss Maynard, as he felt the captain's pulse. "The captain has had another attack—very slight, I assure you—he'll rally from it, I hope, but we must allow nothing to agitate him. There, there, he understands what we say. Don't be cast down, Captain ; God will take care of her, and she has many true friends. It is about you, my dear, he is thinking—I know it by the way his eyes turn towards you."

Clara could no longer restrain her tears, though she tried to conceal them from her father. The doctor's predictions were in part verified : Captain Maynard again rallied sufficiently to make signs for everything he wanted, and showed that his intellect was perfectly clear. With the doctor's permission he received several visits from General Caulfield, though no one else was allowed to see him. Mr. Lerew called frequently. On each occasion he had an interview with Miss Pemberton, and twice he saw Clara, when she was not in attendance on her father. He did his best, as he well knew how, to ingratiate himself with both ladies. He was making way with Miss Pemberton, and hoped that he was gradually winning over Clara. He took good care in her presence to say nothing harsh of General Caulfield, though what he did say was calculated to undermine him in her opinion, but he so cautiously expressed himself that she had no suspicion of the object of his remarks. He managed also never to call when the general was likely to be at the house, as he especially wished to avoid meeting him in the presence of Clara or her aunt. The vicar on three occasions ventured to speak much more openly to Miss Pemberton than he did to Clara.

"What a blessed thing it is, my dear lady, that our Holy Church possesses divinely appointed priests who can unerringly guide and direct their flock; who can rightly administer all the sacraments and interpret the Scriptures! and how sad it is that any should obstinately refuse to take full advantage of all these spiritual blessings!" he remarked. "You and your sweet niece will, I trust, not be among those who thus risk the loss of their souls."

"I hope not," answered Miss Pemberton, becoming somewhat alarmed. "I am sure that I wish to do everything which religion requires."

"There is one great omission of which you have been guilty," continued Mr. Lerew. "I wish to speak with all love and gentleness. You have never yet come to confession."

"Is that necessary?" asked Miss Pemberton, feeling more than ever uneasy. "I did not know that it was required by the Church of England."

"You have read your Prayer Book to

little purpose, if you think so," said Mr. Lerew, with more sternness than he had hitherto shown. "Only think of the unspeakable comfort obtained through priestly absolution, which will be thus afforded you. You will then know that your sins are put away. You will feel so holy, and clean, and pure. Let me, with all loving earnestness, urge you and your sweet niece to come without delay to that holy ordinance, too long ignored and neglected in our Church; and let me assure you that I believe every true daughter of that Church, were she aware of the blessed advantages to be gained, would avail herself of the opportunities now being offered throughout the kingdom."

"Your remarks take me, I own, by surprise," answered Miss Pemberton. "None of my acquaintance, that I am aware of, have ever been in the habit of confessing."

" ' Wide is the gate and broad is the way which leadeth to destruction ; many there be that go in thereat.' Think of that text, Miss Pemberton ; join the privileged few, and I shall be most thankful to receive you as a penitent," answered Mr. Lerew. "Endeavour, also, by all means to induce your niece to follow your pious example. My dear friends, Sir Reginald and Lady Bygrave, and many other persons of distinction, come regularly to confession ; and I trust that by degrees the whole of my flock will take advantage of the opportunity, which I shall have the happiness of offering them, of being absolved from sin."

Miss Pemberton did not exactly say that she would go to confession, as she felt rather doubtful whether Clara would accompany her, but she promised that she would consider the matter; and the vicar on leaving felt satisfied with the way he had made. As yet, however, he had not got so far as to set up a confessional box in his church. He intended, in the first instance, to employ the vestry for that purpose. He had his doubts whether Mr. Lennard might not withdraw the support he was now affording him; still, he had made considerable progress. His first step was to select a dozen of the schoolboys of the parish to form a choir, and to clothe them in surplices; the instruments which had hitherto led the parishioners in their singing being banished, an organ, presented by Lady Bygrave, was put up, and an organist with high ritualistic proclivities appointed. The hymn-books with the good old tunes which all the parish knew by heart were discarded, and Hymns Ancient and Modern were introduced. The communion-table was next raised and adorned with a richly embroidered cover, and on the following Sunday four magnificent branch candlesticks appeared upon it. Mr. Lennard had hitherto not made any remarks on the alterations going forward; but when he saw the candlesticks, he enquired of Mr. Lerew, who was calling on him, what funds he possessed for the purchase of such articles, and what was their object, as he feared that they would not be appreciated by the parishioners at large.

"I have ample funds for all such purposes; and ignorant as the people are at present, we will so educate them that by degrees they will see the value and significance of the improvements we are introducing," answered Mr. Lerew;

"I contemplate having a reredos erected, which will add greatly to the beauty of the church; as it will be expensive, I own, I trust that you and other friends will contribute from your means towards the important work. I wish to ornament those blank spaces along the aisle with appropriate pictures. I should prefer having them painted on the walls, of medallion shape; but as it may be difficult to get an artist down here, we must be content to have them in moveable frames. I purpose also having a large picture of the Crucifixion, or perhaps one of the Holy Virgin, put up over the altar, instead of the Ten Commandments, which greatly offend my eye; while I confess that I cannot consider the altar complete without the symbol of our faith placed on it. I should have preferred a crucifix of full size, and I think that the cross might be so arranged that the figure can at any time be added ; but I fear that at present some of the parishioners in their ignorance might raise objections which would cause us some trouble."

" I should think, indeed, that they would object ! " exclaimed Mr. Lennard. " Are you not going on too fast ? I do not complain that your improvements cast some reflection on me ; as being a mere *locum tenens*, I could not have made the alterations you propose, even had I wished to do so ; but others might find very great fault with you."

" You will come over fully to agree with me, as my kind friends Sir Reginald and Lady Bygrave have done," said the vicar, and with a gentle smile he bid his host good-bye.

Scarcely had Mr. Lerew gone than a

note was brought to Mr. Lennard, from Lady Bygrave, requesting him, with his son and daughter, to spend a few days at Swanston Hall. Lady Bygrave was a very charming person, and pleasant people were generally to be met with at the Hall. He gladly accepted the invitation. Alfred was delighted ; Mary would rather have gone back to stay with Clara.

Mr. Lennard was somewhat surprised to find that the abbé and Father Lascelles were still there. "The friends to whom they were going were unable to receive them, and Sir Reginald requested them to stay on as long as they found it convenient," remarked Lady Bygrave. Mr. Lennard was disappointed at finding no one else at the house, with the exception of a young lady rather older than Mary, of grave and sedate manners. As she was dressed in black, Mr. Lennard concluded that she was in mourning for a parent or some other near relative, which accounted for the gravity of one so young. She, however, smiled very sweetly when Mary was introduced to her, and said in a gentle voice, " I know that we shall become good friends, so pray let us begin at once, and talk to each other without reserve."

Mr. Lennard, who had often wished that Mary could enjoy the companionship of a girl of her own age, was glad to find so apparently amiable a young lady in the house. The abbé, on entering the room, expressed his pleasure at seeing Mr. Lennard, and certainly did his best to make amends for the want of other society. Father Lascelles, observing that Alfred did not know what to do with himself, proposed taking a turn round the grounds. " I am not much of a sportsman," he said as they walked on, "but I am fond of fishing, as I dare say you are, and we will fish together to-morrow, if you like." He had discovered that angling—an art in which he was an adept in more ways than one—was the only amusement which suited Alfred's tastes.

The few days spent at the Hall went rapidly by. At first the abbé carefully avoided any but secular subjects, and being a remarkably well-informed man, he made himself very agreeable. Even when Sir Reginald or Lady Bygrave seemed inclined to speak on religion, he quickly turned the conversation, but by degrees he, with apparent unwillingness, entered into matters of faith. Mr. Lennard, who had never given any attention to the Papal system, was surprised to find how little, according to the abbé's showing, the Church of

England differed from that of Rome in all matters of importance.

"Ah," remarked the abbé, with a smile, "your Church is like a wandering child—though you have gone away from the parent, you retain all your main features and doctrines, and have but to own obedience to the chief head, and you would again be one with us. What a happy consummation! Would that it were brought about! Why should those of the same kindred be divided?"

"It is sad that it should be so," remarked Lady Bygrave, "perhaps, if His Holiness, the Pope, were not so exigeant in his demands, the glorious union might soon be accomplished."

"It is there that you are in error, my dear lady," remarked the abbé, blandly; "His Holiness is too loving a parent to be exigeant without good reason. Think of the parable of the Prodigal Son—what a warm welcome! what rich treasures the father had for him, who was willing to return! such as all will experience who, having eaten of the husks of Protestantism, fly back to the bosom of the mother-Church."

Mr. Lennard above all things hated an argument, and would always rather side with a companion than oppose him; still he was not won by the sophisms of the abbé; but he did not, unhappily, reflect on the effect they might produce on Alfred and Mary. He had studied the Thirty-nine Articles when he had taken his ordination vows, and he saw that the opinions expressed by Lady Bygrave, and occasionally by Sir Reginald, who was even more open than his wife, could not be reconciled to them. The abbé never uttered a word which showed that he considered there were any material differences in the two creeds, with the exception of the single one of want of obedience to the heads of the Church.

"You have simplified your services; you have eliminated several doctrines which we consider of importance; but such doctrines are, I rejoice to see, in the course of being rapidly restored to their proper position, as are many of the practices and observances of our Holy Church," said the abbé, "and all you have now to say is, I will return, I will obey, and the union is complete."

"You make the matter certainly very easy," said Mr. Lennard; "but having been for forty years of my life accustomed to consider that there is a much wider gap between our Churches than that you have so quickly passed over, you must not

be surprised if I hesitate to take the leap ;
but I will consider the subject."

"Far be it from me to advise you
to do what your conscience might disap-
prove," observed the abbé.

Father Lascelles found that he could
be more open with Alfred. His chief
aim was to impress upon the young
man's mind that there was but one true
Church, and that of Rome being the most
ancient and most powerful, and holding
out unspeakably greater advantages to its
followers, must be that true one. Still,
Alfred was neither very impressive not
communicative ; the Jesuit priest could
draw no positive conclusion as to the
effect his remarks had produced, though
he felt sure that, could he obtain time to
play the fish he had hooked, he should
land him safe at last.

Mary's friend, Emmeline Tracy, was

unexpectedly called away from the Hall.
Even to Mary she did not say where she
was going, as she bid her good-bye,
but she hoped, she said, ere long to see
her again. Mr. Lennard observed that
his daughter looked more thoughtful and
in less good spirits than usual; it reminded
him of his often expressed determination
of sending her to a finishing school, that
she might have the benefit of young companions, and form pleasant friendships.
He mentioned his idea to Lady Bygrave.

"By all means, Mr. Lennard; it is
what I should strongly recommend,"
answered her ladyship. "It is curious
that I was thinking of the same thing.
There is a school at Cheltenham exactly
of the character you would wish for your
daughter. Mrs. Barnett, the mistress, is
a lady of high attainments and amiable
disposition, and she receives only girls

of the first families ; so that Mary would be certain of forming desirable acquaintances. I shall have great pleasure in writing to Mrs. Barnett, saying who you are, and requesting her to receive your daughter directly she has a vacancy."

Mr. Lennard returned home ; and a few days afterwards Lady Bygrave sent him a letter from Mrs. Barnett, who said, that in consequence of the very satisfactory account her ladyship had written of Mr. Lennard and his daughter, she should be happy to receive the young lady as an inmate immediately, to fill up the only vacancy in her establishment, and which she regretted that she could not keep open beyond a week or so."

"Let me earnestly advise you to send Mary at once," added her ladyship. "It would be a grievous pity to lose so favourable an opportunity of placing her in a satisfactory school; for good schools are, I know, rare enough."

Mr. Lennard accordingly made up his mind to take his daughter to Cheltenham. Mary had only time to drive over and pay a short visit to Clara.

"I hope you will be happy," said Clara. " As I never was at school, I don't know what sort of life you will have to lead, but I should think with the companionship of a number of nice girls it must be very cheerful. You can never for a moment feel out of spirits for want of society, as I do too often here, now that I am unable to converse with my poor father, and you know that Aunt Sarah is not the most entertaining of persons."

Mary went away in good spirits, promising to write to Clara, and tell her all about the school. Mr. Lennard and his daughter arrived safely at Cheltenham, and

reached Mrs. Barnett's handsome mansion.
Everything about it appeared to be as he
could desire; the sitting-rooms were well
furnished, and the bedroom his daughter
was to occupy with several other girls
looked remarkably comfortable, the walls
being adorned with pictures, of which,
however, he did not take much notice,
though he saw by a glance he gave at
them that they were Scripture subjects.
As they were passing along a passage,
the mistress hastily closed a door, but not
until he observed at the farther end of the
room a table, on which stood vases of
flowers and candlesticks surmounted by
what looked very like a crucifix; but he
was too polite to interrogate Mrs. Barnett
on the subject, and she evidently did not
intend that he should look into the room.
To most of his inquiries he received satisfactory answers: the young ladies attended

church regularly, and were visited and catechised periodically by a clergyman in whose judgment and piety Mrs. Barnett said she had the most perfect confidence. Poor Mary threw her arms round her father's neck as he was taking his leave, and burst into tears.

"I wish that I had not come, papa," she whispered. "I don't know why, but I can't bear the thoughts of parting from you."

He endeavoured to comfort her, and consoled himself that he had acted for the best, though it cost him much to leave his little girl in the hands of strangers.

He had another duty to perform, less trying to his feelings, however. It was to take Alfred up to Oxford. Alfred had specially requested to be allowed to go to —— College, which, though not enjoying the fame of older institutions, Alfred averred that he should feel more at home at than in any other. He was duly introduced to the head of his college, where rooms were allotted to him, and forthwith matriculating, he became an undergraduate. Mr. Lennard, believing that he had performed his duty, left his son to make his way as thousands of young men have had to do before him.

Chapter III.

CLARA was seated in the drawing-room. She had just written a long letter to Harry, in which she told him of the various events which had taken place in the neighbourhood. She wrote unreservedly, describing, among other persons, Mr. and Mrs. Lerew, and the constant attention and kindness they had shown her. She naturally spoke of the church, and of the various improvements, as she called them, which had been introduced. "Nothing can be more elegant than the reredos which our excellent vicar has erected at his own expense," she wrote.

" The altar, too, is beautifully adorned, and the music, considering the performers, is wonderfully good ; for Mrs. Lerew has taken great pains to instruct the choir, and we occasionally have a first-rate musician from London to lead them ; while an air of solemnity pervades the service, both on Sundays and week-days, very different to anything we have before had in this neighbourhood." She did not say that she went to confession, but she remarked that she derived great comfort from the spiritual advice of the vicar. The letter was closed ready for the post, when General Caulfield was announced. He came to bid her and her father a hurried farewell, as he had just been summoned by telegram to the north of England, to the bedside of a dying brother, whose executor he was, and he greatly feared that some time might clapse before he should be able to return.

"I wish to suggest to you, my dear Clara, before I go," he said, "that it will be well, in the position in which you are placed, to avoid too great an intimacy with the vicar and his wife, of whose constant visits to you I have heard. He may be, according to his own notions, a religious man, but he is not acting faithfully to the Church of which he is a minister. He has already made many innovations in this parish which are contrary to the spirit and practice of that Protestant Church, and, from what I hear and observe, he intends to make others; while he has openly preached several Romish doctrines, and I see his name among the members of the Church Union, which avowedly repudiates Protestant principles. I am sure that Harry would give you the advice I do, and I deeply regret that I cannot remain to afford you any assistance you may require."

A blush rose on Clara's brow. She could not openly express any disagreement with the general, but she thought he was harsh and illiberal in the opinion he had uttered. She replied that she had already written to Harry, and told him all about the church and the vicar, and hoped that he would not find any great fault with her.

The general appeared satisfied. He remained but a short time with his poor friend, whom he believed that he should never again see on earth; for he remarked, what Clara had failed to do, the great change in her father's countenance since his last visit. He took an affectionate farewell of his intended daughter-in-law and, not being aware of the influence the vicar had already obtained over her and her aunt, he did not further warn her against him. Still, he left her with some anxious forebodings, regretting the stern necessity which compelled him to be away from her at the time when his advice might be of so much importance. The general's absence was felt by others in the parish ; he was looked upon as the person best calculated, from his position and truly Christian character, to lead those desirous of opposing the ritualistic practices introduced by the new vicar, which were already making rapid progress. The general had been faithfully attached to the establishment ; he had gone, as usual, to the parish church, in spite of the introduction of the surpliced choir, of "Hymns Ancient and Modern," the richly adorned communion table, and several other additions which had been cautiously introduced ; but when he heard from the lips of the vicar the doctrine of transubstantiation clearly and unmistakably enounced, and afterwards saw him habited in a robe resembling that of a Romish priest elevate the elements, he felt compelled to absent himself, and on the next Sunday to attend the service at a Congregational chapel. He had, in in the meantime, expostulated with Mr. Lerew, both personally and by letter, but had received only a curt and unsatisfactory reply. He had afterwards heard, from undoubted authority, that the doctrine of purgatory was taught to the school-children ; that prayers for the dead were offered up, as also prayers to the Virgin Mary ; that the saints were invoked ; that a font had been placed at the entrance of the church for the reception of holy water. A considerable number of the parishioners had for some time withdrawn themselves from the church ; Lieutenant Sims had declared that he would never enter it to listen to Mr. Lerew, after he had heard him say that the Bible was a dangerous book. Many sided with the lieutenant; others asserted that he must have misunderstood the vicar—he could not have uttered such an opinion ; some even went so far as to say Mr. Sims had through envy, hatred, and malice stated what he knew to be a falsehood. The lieutenant, supported by his wife, boldly adhered to what he had said ; the parishioners were by the ears on the subject. Miss Pemberton had been appealed to, but declared she could not understand what Mr. Lerew had said, and her evidence went rather against Mr. Sims; but when candles and flowers appeared on the altar, and a rich cross rose above it, and the vicar, habited in new-fangled

robes, turned his back on the congregation, the partisans of the gallant lieutenant
increased, and each innovation introduced
by the vicar brought Mr. Sims a fresh
accession of supporters. They talked
seriously of building another church,
and made arrangements to apply to the
bishop; but it was found that both parties
were so scattered over the two parishes,
which were of very considerable extent,
that their object was unattainable. While
General Caulfield remained among them,
he prevented the flame of discord from
bursting forth. He allowed no angry
word to escape his lips, but contented
himself with simply preaching the Gospel,
either in the Congregational Chapel on a
week-day evening, or in a large barn he
had hired and fitted up for the purpose
of holding meetings. It was always full,
and many came from the farther end of

the parish. Calm and calculating as
Mr. Lerew generally was, he became ex-
cessively indignant on hearing of this;
but he considered the general too important a person to be attacked personally, though he spoke everywhere in the
strongest terms of his unwarrantable conduct, denominating him as a schismatic of
the worst description. Great was his satisfaction when he heard that the general
had gone away. He now fancied that he
could carry on his proceedings without
opposition. He was mistaken, however;
for Lieutenant Sims and his party ceased
not to protest against all he did; and
petitions were sent to the bishop, who,
however, if he did not encourage Mr.
Lerew's proceedings, took no steps to
put a stop to them. Mr. Lennard was
appealed to, but he declined to interfere,
declaring that he saw nothing so very

objectionable in the changes which had been made; and as to doctrines, the vicar of the parish was more likely to know what was right or wrong than the parishioners whom he came to teach.

" In my opinion, our late vicar is as bad as the present one," exclaimed Lieutenant Sims ; " but how the poor man, whom all thought so much of, has been so completely bamboozled is more than I can tell."

Mr. Lerew had lately, by the advice of Lady Bygrave, designed a grand scheme. It was the establishment of a college or school for eighty young ladies in the parish, for whose accommodation handsome buildings were to be erected ; and Lady Bygrave, with other ladies of consequence in the county, undertook to be patronesses. In his prospectus Mr. Lerew dwelt especially on the importance of young ladies being carefully trained in religious principles, and removed from the pernicious influence of unauthorised instructors ; whereas at St. Agatha's they would be placed under the direct super-intendence of their lawful priests, and instructed in catholic doctrine. Lady Bygrave had already recommended as mother-superior a lady of great piety and experience, and the teachers were to be sisters of the community of St. Mary the Virgin, in the neighbouring town of Bansfield, who were celebrated for their truly religious and self-denying lives. The young ladies, thus judiciously trained, would, it was hoped, become the mothers of England's future legislators, and mate-rially contribute to the establishment of catholic principles throughout the land. Mr. Lerew had, however, another pro-spectus more generally circulated among those of whose principles he was uncertain, and in which he simply set forth that an excellent first-class school was about to be established for the benefit of their own and neighbouring counties, and asking for subscriptions and support to so desirable an institution. Subscriptions, however, did not come in with the same rapidity as he had hoped, and he saw that he must employ other means for raising the necessary funds. Mrs. Lerew wrote to all her more wealthy acquaintances, and Lady Bygrave was, as usual, most liberal. Few of the parishioners would subscribe, with the exception of some of the principal tradesmen, who hoped to do business with the new establishment, Mr. Rowe, an apothecary, who expected to be employed as medical attendant, and the solicitor who had been engaged in making the legal arrangements.

People had begun to grow suspicious of the vicar, and even of Lady Bygrave, in consequence of the long stay at the Hall of the abbé and Father Lascelles. Lady Bygrave did her utmost to maintain her popularity by incessantly driving about and visiting the houses of the better-to-do people and the cottages of the poor, much as she would have done on an electioneering canvass. She was, of course, politely received by all classes; but though she won over some, a large number of people were too sound Protestants to be influenced by her plausible and attractive manners. It would have been happy for poor Clara and her Aunt Sarah, had they been equally on their guard. Miss Pemberton, indeed, declared that whatever so charming a person as Lady Bygrave did must be right, and she now not only attended all the services at the church on Sundays and week-days, but induced Clara to accompany her. Though Clara went, she often felt that it was her duty to be watching by the bedside of her father; she, indeed, sometimes begged on that plea to remain at home.

" But, my dear, your duties to God and the commands of our Holy Church are superior to those you owe to a human parent, and you should therefore not allow yourself to be influenced by the natural affections of your heart," observed Miss Pemberton, using the argument she had previously learned from Mr. Lerew.

Clara had been absent at one of these week-day services, and the vicar had promised to call and have some conversation with her and her aunt, when on her return she observed an expression of subdued sorrow and alarm on the countenances of the servants.

"Is my father worse?" she asked anxiously; and before any one could stop her, she rushed upstairs, and entered Captain Maynard's room. She approached the bed. There was no movement—his eyes were closed, and the nurse was standing by the bedside—her father was dead. She knew it at once, and as she leant over him, she sank fainting on his inanimate body. Miss Pemberton, having learned the truth, quickly followed, and directed that she should be carried from the room. On the application of restoratives Clara revived; but scarcely had she returned to consciousness than Mr. Lerew drove up to the door. Though he was told what had happened, he insisted on seeing Miss Maynard.

"As a priest, I can afford her spiritual

comfort and support," he said, almost forcing his way in. Miss Pemberton, not daring to decline his visit, ushered him into Clara's room. He took a seat by her side. He spoke softly and gently.

"We must look at what has happened as a dispensation of heaven," he remarked; "but though, unhappily, your father to the last refused the ordinances of our Church, I am fain to believe that he did so under malign influence, and from weakness of mind induced by sickness. It is a consolation to know that prayers continually offered in his behalf by a true votaress to the loving Mother of God can in time release him from the condition in which I fear he is placed. With what thankfulness you should receive this glorious doctrine, my dear Miss Maynard! what calm should it bring to your troubled heart! I will not fail, believe me, to offer the prayers of the Church for the same object; and if you did but consider their efficacy, you would cease to mourn as you now do."

Poor Clara was too completely overwhelmed by grief to understand the meaning of what the vicar said, though she heard the words issuing from his mouth.

" I will relieve you," he continued, "from all the painful arrangements connected with the funeral, in conjunction with your aunt, whom I will now join in the drawing-room."

" Oh! thank you! thank you!" exclaimed Clara, between her sobs. " I shall be most grateful—do whatever you think best."

Mr. Lerew retired; and after a conversation of some length with Miss Pemberton he drove away. Clara—so absorbing was her grief—could with difficulty regain her power of thought. She felt alone in the world. Had General Caulfield been at home, she would have had him to consult; but she had no confidence in her Aunt Sarah's judgment, though she had of late been more guided by her than she was aware of.

" Our excellent vicar and I have arranged everything," said Miss Pemberton, on entering the room some time afterwards ; "so do not further trouble yourself about the matter."

Clara expressed her thanks to her aunt. Completely prostrate, she remained in bed. Workmen sent by the vicar came to the house, and were employed for some time in her father's room. She dared not inquire what they were about. At length she arose and dressed. She felt a longing desire once more to gaze on those dear features. She inquired whether she might go to the room.

"Oh, yes, miss," was the answer. "It's all done up on purpose, and looks so grand."

She hurried on, and, entering, what was her astonishment to find the room draped in black, the windows closed, and several long wax candles arranged round the bed on which her father's body lay, dressed in his naval uniform. She approached, and leant over the bed, on which, after standing gazing at his features for some minutes, she sank down with her arms extended, almost fainting. At that instant the vicar appeared at the doorway.

"What a lovely picture!" he whispered, as if to himself; "can anything surpass it?"

Clara heard him, and had still strength sufficient to rise.

"We have done what we can to do honour to your father," he said, advancing and taking her hand. "Had General Caulfield been present, we should have been prevented from making these arrangements; and I lay all the blame of Captain Maynard's neglect of the sacred ordinances on him, as I am sure it will be laid at the day of judgment; therefore, my sweet young lady, I would urge you to mourn not as those without hope. I come to console and sympathise with you. Let me lead you from the room, as others are anxious to pay their last respects to your parent; it will be trying to your feelings to receive them."

Clara submitted, and was led by the vicar into the drawing-room, where she found her aunt. Mr. Lerew now became more cheerful in his conversation, and spoke of his new college, and of a

society of Anglican sisters of mercy, in
which he was deeply interested. He
enlarged on their pious, self-denying
labours, so admirably adapted to distract
the minds of the sorrowing from worldly
cares and the thoughts of the past, and
the charming qualities of the lady superior,
and of the calm happiness enjoyed by all
under her rule.

"You will find subjects for consideration
in these volumes," said Mr. Lerew, taking
two books from his pocket; "the one
describes fully the joys of a religious life,
and the other points out to you rules for
your daily government. Your aunt has
already several works I left with her some
time ago, to which I would also draw your
attention; and may they prove a blessing
to your soul."

Saying this, the vicar took his leave.
In the meantime several persons had

come to the house; and scarcely had the vicar left the room than the voice of Mr. Sims was heard exclaiming, " By whose authority, I should like to know, has the deathbed of my poor friend been sur- rounded by those popish play-acting mummeries which I witnessed just now? He was one of the last men on earth who would have sanctioned such proceedings."

" Sir, sir!" exclaimed Mr. Lerew in an angry tone, " I scarcely understand your meaning; but if you allude to the arrange- ments in the chamber of death above, I have to inform you that they were made by those who had ample authority for doing as they thought right; and I have to add that I consider your remarks in- decorous and highly impertinent."

" I differ with you on that point," answered the lieutenant, restraining his anger; "and I only hope my poor friend's daughter has had nothing to do with the matter. It signifies very little to him, or I believe he'd get up and capsize all the candles, and cut down the black cloth rigged round his bed. Why, I'm as sure as I am of my own existence that he died like a true Christian, and is now in the glorious realms of the blest, or I don't know what the Gospel means. What does he want with all that black stuff round him? It's just robbing the orphan to put money in the pockets of the undertakers. And now you've got my opinion, I'll wish you good morning;" and Mr. Sims walked out of the house, leaving the vicar fuming and boiling with unwonted rage.

Mr. Sims had intended leaving a message expressive of his and his wife's sympathy for poor Clara; but his indignation at what he had witnessed very naturally threw everything else out of his head. He notwithstanding attended Captain Maynard's funeral, which was conducted with more ceremonies than had ever yet taken place in the parish. Numerous carriages followed the hearse, and the procession formed in the church walked after the coffin, the individuals forming it surrounding the grave, chanting a requiem as the coffin was committed to its last resting-place.

The vicar had kept secret the last interview he had had with Captain Maynard, who, he let it be supposed, had gone through all the required ordinances of the Church before the last seizure, which had deprived him of the power of speech. Those who knew the captain best averred that he would never have consented to the performance in his presence of any Romish ceremony, and that the vicar had some object in view in allowing the idea to get abroad. The parish became more divided than ever, but the original cause of dispute held its ground, and those who sided with the vicar would no longer visit or speak to those who believed that he had declared the Bible to be a dangerous book.

Clara's grief for the loss of her father was sincere and deep. Her nature was one requiring such consolation as a sympathising friend could afford. Her aunt was never sympathising or gentle, and she had become still less so since she had attended the frequent services of the Church. Early rising did not suit her constitution; but though she thoroughly disliked it, she considered it her duty to induce her niece to accompany her.

Thus time went on at Luton. General Caulfield was detained in the North; he wrote frequently to Clara. Not aware of the influences to which she was exposed, he did not mention the vicar, and failed to caution her, as he otherwise would have done. She, knowing his opinions, did not venture to tell him all that was occur ring, though he saw by the tone of her letters that she was unhappy and ill at ease from some cause or other, besides the natural grief she felt for the loss of her father, and her anxiety about Harry. She had heard of his arrival, and that his regiment was ordered up the country, but she had received no answer to the letter she wrote, describing the services at the church, and the various changes introduced by the vicar. Her aunt had, in the meantime, become less agreeable and communicative even than before. She was constantly absorbed in the books lent her by Mr. Lerew, and she very frequently drove over to the vicarage to see him.

Clara had at first felt but little interest in the two works he had presented to her; she had glanced over their pages, and was somewhat startled at the language used and the advice given in them, so different to that to which she had been accustomed. On one of his visits he inquired whether she had studied them, and she had to confess the truth. He then entreated her not to risk her spiritual welfare by any longer neglecting to read the works so calculated to advance it. She promised to follow his advice. Had Clara known more of the world, and possessed more self-reliance, her eyes might have been opened by what she read ; but she wanted some one to lean on, and on her aunt's judgment she had no reliance. The vicar appeared, from his position and serious manner, to be the person in whom she ought to confide. Had the general been at Luton, she would have gone to him; but she could not write what she might have spoken; and she finally gave herself up to the guidance of Mr. Lerew, as her aunt had long since done.

The following Sunday the communion was to be held, or, as the vicar expressed it, the Holy Eucharist was to be celebrated; "But," he added, "I have made it a rule that I will administer it to none who have not made confession and received that absolution I am authorised to grant."

"I was not aware of that," said Clara; "how long has that rule existed?"

"I have only lately made it," he replied, "and from it I cannot depart."

Clara hesitated; but her aunt, who had several times gone to confession, assured her that there was nothing in it very terrible, and overcame her scruples. Clara promised to go. It was held in the vestry, one person at a time only being admitted. The questions asked and the answers given cannot be repeated. Clara, as she knelt leaning on a chair in front of the priest, could with difficulty support herself; her heart felt bursting; she was nearly fainting; the colour mounted to her cheeks and brow; she could not lift her eyes from the ground towards the man who was questioning her. More than once she was inclined to rise and flee from the room rather than continue to undergo the mental torture she was suffering. Never afterwards did she look the vicar in the face. At length the ordeal was over, the *Te absolvo* was pronounced, and she, with trembling knees, hanging down her head, tottered to her pew by the side of her aunt, where she knelt to conceal her features, while uncontrollable sobs burst from her bosom.

"What's the matter?" whispered Miss Pemberton. "Take my smelling-bottle. Don't let people hear you; they'll fancy there must be something very dreadful."

The music that day was unusually good. Several first-rate performers had been engaged to attend, with three or four clergymen from various parts of the county. They, in their richest robes, glittering with embroidery, walked round the church. There were the acolytes with lighted candles, the thurifer, with the cross-bearer, and others carrying banners; while the organ played, and the fumes of incense filled the church. Clara's agitation ceased, but no peace was brought to her soul. She returned home with her aunt, humbled and more wretched than she had ever before felt in her life.

Chapter IV.

MONDAY morning brought Clara Harry's looked-for letter. She hurried with it to her room. It was full of love and tenderness, but Harry expressed his regret at hearing of the changes which had been made in the church, and still more of the ritualistic practices of the new vicar.

"I need scarcely urge you, dearest, not to be inveigled by them," he continued, "as I have often said I cannot conceive a man in his senses marrying a girl who has submitted to the abominable confession—it must ultimately deprave her mind, and prevent her from placing that confidence in her husband which he has a right to expect; while it proves her ignorance of one of the most vital truths of our holy faith, that we have a High Priest in heaven, who knows our infirmities, and is touched by our sorrows, and who is more tender and loving than any human being, and is ever ready to receive those who come to Him. Oh! do warn any girls of your acquaintance not to yield to the sophistries which would persuade them that Christ allows a human being to stand in His stead between Himself and the sinner. It is one of the numberless devices of Satan to rob Him of the honour and love which are His due. We are told when we have offended a fellow mortal to confess our fault, and to ask pardon; but we are emphatically charged to confess our sins to God alone,

trusting to the all-sufficient atonement
made once for all for us by Christ on
Calvary, and through His mediation we
are assured of perfect forgiveness. These
impious sacerdotalists, for the sake of
gaining influence over the minds of those
they hope to deceive, step in, and daringly
arrogate to themselves the position which
our loving Lord desires alone to hold.
But I must not continue the subject—I
know that it is not necessary to say this
to you. Should you ever be perplexed,
or require assistance, I am sure that you
will apply to my kind and excellent
father, who is ever anxious to treat you
as a beloved daughter."

Clara read the letter with burning
cheek.

"Oh, what have I done!" she exclaimed; "I am unworthy of the confidence
he places in me." Directly afterwards she

tried to find an excuse for herself. "Perhaps he is mistaken in his ideas ; and Mr. Lerew says that the general is a schismatic, and Harry has imbibed his views. I dare not refuse to obey the voice of the Church, and Mr. Lerew tells me that that insists on confession before absolution can be granted, and without absolution we cannot partake of the Holy Eucharist."

Such was her line of thought, and she determined to try and persuade Harry to agree with her. She sat down and wrote to him, quoting several passages from the books lent to her by the vicar. She implored him seriously to consider the matter, and not to imperil his soul by refusing obedience to the Church. So eager did she become as she warmed in her subject, that she forgot to put in those affectionate expressions which her previous letter had contained. No sooner had the epistle been despatched than she began to regret having said some things in it and omitted others. She tried to think over its contents; as she did so she became more and more dissatisfied. At last she resolved to write another, to confess that she was sorry she had written the first, to tell Harry of her difficulties, and to ask his advice. Her aunt came in just as she had closed it, and offered to post it for her. That letter never reached its destination.

Poor Clara, agitated by conflicting emotions, and all her previous opinions upset, at last thought of writing to General Caulfield, telling him of all her doubts and troubles, that perhaps he might see things in the light in which the vicar presented them. Miss Pemberton found the letter on the hall table, and suspecting its contents, took it to the vicar, who advised that it should not be forwarded. Clara in vain waited for a reply; no letters reached her from the general, and she ultimately came to the conclusion that he was so much offended with her for what she had said, that he would write no more.

Week after week passed by, and no letter came from Harry.

"Can he have cast me off because I show an anxiety about my spiritual welfare?" she exclaimed, somewhat bitterly to herself. "Mr. Lerew must be right when he speaks of the bigotry of the Evangelical party."

Mr. Lerew called the next day, and spoke pathetically of the trials to which the true sons and daughters of the Church must expect to be exposed; and left some tracts, which especially pointed out the holy delights of a convent life; one, indeed, declared that the only sure way by which a woman could avoid the trials and troubles of the present evil world and gain eternal happiness was by entering a convent and devoting herself to the service of religion. Clara read them over and over, and sighed often. Miss Pemberton expressed her high approval of them.

" I am, indeed, my dear niece, contemplating myself becoming a Sister of Charity, and only regret that I was not led in early life to do so—how many wasted days of idleness and frivolity I might have avoided." Miss Pemberton did not like to speak of years.

The vicar, who had now become an almost daily visitor, just then appeared. He held forth eloquently on the subject of which the ladies had been speaking ; a friend of his, a most charming, delightful person, was the Lady Superior of one of the oldest and most devoted sisterhoods which had been established in England since, as he expressed it, true Catholic principles had been revived in the Church. He was sure that no lady could do otherwise than rejoice to the end of her days, who should become a member of her community. The Sisters were employed in numerous meritorious works of charity; he had hoped that Miss Maynard would take an active part in St. Agatha's College; but some time must probably elapse before more than a very limited number of teachers could find occupation, and he besides doubted whether she would find the duties of an instructress suited to her taste.

"I should not, I fear, find my powers equal to them," answered Clara, humbly; "and yet I have a longing for some occupation in the service of the Church. Such means as I possess, however, I would gladly devote to the establishment of St. Agatha's."

"Ah, my dear young lady, I rejoice to hear you say that," exclaimed Mr. Lerew. "Whatever you give, you give to the Church, remember, and she has promised to repay you a hundredfold."

Mrs. Lerew frequently called on Clara, as also did Lady Bygrave. Both spoke enthusiastically of the holy and happy life of Sisters of Mercy, and still more so of those nuns who gave themselves up to religious meditation. Lady Bygrave, especially, warmly pressed the subject on Clara's consideration.

"Were I young, I should certainly devote myself to a religious life; but as I am married, my husband might raise objections," she remarked.

Clara thought and thought on all she heard, and became more and more interested in the books her advisers put into her hands. She resolved, however, to wait before deciding till she received a letter from Harry. She could not easily give him up; and she hoped, when she should be his wife, to win him over to support the cause of the Church, whicl. she persuaded herself would be as accept· able to Heaven as should she become a nun.

While Clara had gone one day to return a visit from Lady Bygrave, Miss Pemberton received and opened the post-bag. It contained a letter for Clara from India. She saw that it was from Harry. She turned it over several times.

"I must obey my spiritual adviser," she said to herself; "it can do the child no harm."

Replacing several other letters for Clara, she took this one up into her own room. She had been instructed how carefully to open letters by the vicar, for he had been at an English school, and having been taught in his boyhood to consider breaking the seal of another person's letter a disgraceful act, was glad to escape it. After a little time she succeeded in reaching the enclosure. She glanced over the first portion.

"A part of your letter, dearest one, though I delight in hearing from you, gave me great pain. I had hoped and believed that you were better grounded in the fundamental truths of the Gospel than to express yourself as you have done. You speak of Holy Church as if there were one visible establishment on earth which all are bound to obey, when Christ founded only one spiritual Church, on the great truth enunciated by Peter, that He was the Christ, the Son of the living God. From that time forward, throughout the whole of the New Testament, no other Church is spoken of. Churches or assemblies existed, founded by the apostles, but they were independent of each other, and were solely united by having one faith and one allegiance to one great head, Jesus Christ ; but in such simple forms as were introduced for the convenience of public worship they materially differed from each other. Under the new covenant no material temple or worldly sanctuary exists ; the old covenant had ordinances of divine service and of worldly sanctuary, but these, the apostle tells us, have waxed old and vanished away, Christ being come, the High Priest of good things to come, by a greater and more perfect tabernacle not made with hands ; and he assures us that the only temple now existing is

the spiritual Church of the living God.
" Know ye not that ye are the temple of
God, and that the Spirit of God dwelleth
in you? ye also as lively stones are built
up a spiritual house, a holy priesthood, to
offer up spiritual sacrifices to God by
Jesus Christ, whose house are ye, Jesus
Christ Himself being the chief corner-
stone ; " and our Lord Himself tells us that
where two or three are gathered together,
even there is He in their midst. The
priest, the sacrifice, the altar, and the
temple of the old covenant were only
types of the good things to come under
the Gospel. When Christ ascended on
high, all human priesthood was abolished;
our only priestly mediator or intercessor
is Jesus Christ, the one Mediator between
God and men, who is the one righteous
Advocate, the one ever-living Intercessor,
and His glory will He not give to

another, He who has once suffered for sinners, the just for the unjust, that He might bring us to God. The apostles themselves never assumed the character of priests ; they pointed to the Great High Priest, Jesus Christ the righteous, and would have looked upon it as blasphemy for any man to presume to act as such. To our Great High Priest alone must we confess our sins ; He is faithful and just to forgive all those their sins, who put faith in the all-cleansing power of His blood to absolve them. He, too, is One who knows our infirmities, and can sympathise with us, having been tempted as we are. With the Scriptures in our hands, we need no mortal man to declare this glorious truth to us; and knowing it, we can come boldly to the throne of grace, and He is ever ready to receive all who come to Him. All the forms and

9

ceremonies, the embellishments which you describe, are but imitations of those of the Church of Rome, which are themselves taken from the ceremonies of the old heathen temples, with large admixtures from those of the Jews. From the earliest times, Satan has induced men to assume the character of priests, for the purpose of deceiving their fellow-creatures. The same spirit exists at the present day; and as he can become an angel of light in appearance, so may those men who thus blasphemously take the name of priests appear pure and holy in the sight of those whom they deceive. Let me entreat you, my beloved Clara, to break from the chains which have been thrown around you. Seek for grace and strength from above, and consult my kind father. Tell him frankly all that the vicar has endeavoured to teach you to believe, and I feel assured that he will thoroughly satisfy your mind."

Harry said more to the same effect.

" It will never do for Clara to see this letter," thought Miss Pemberton; " I must take it to Mr. Lerew, and ascertain what he thinks."

She set off at once, that she might get to the vicarage and back before Clara's return. The vicar read it with knitted brow.

" You did right, my dear sister," he said; " it might defeat all our plans. Far better commit it to the flames. Let me think—will you permit me to take possession of the letter? good may result from it; the end, as you know, my dear lady, sanctifies the means."

" Whatever you consider right, I of course will do," said Miss Pemberton, giving the letter, which with the envelope the vicar put into his desk; and the lady hastened home.

"It is the aunt's doing, not mine," he muttered to himself; "but were the poor girl to receive this abominable production, it might destroy the result of all the training I have given her. No priest! no sacrifice! no confession! no power of absolution! What would become of the Church—what of us—if such principles were to regain their ascendancy over the minds of the people? These abominable evangelical notions must be crushed by every means in our power, or the efforts which for years we have made to introduce Catholic doctrine would be utterly lost. We must get the girl without delay to enter a convent, and the sooner she is induced to do so the better."

Mr. Lerew waited for some days before he paid Clara another visit. She had discovered that the Indian post had come in, and had brought her, as she supposed, no letter from Harry. She began to imagine all sorts of things ; she saw that there were accounts of engagements with the hill-tribes—could he have gone up the country with a detachment of his regiment? or perhaps her letter had so offended him that he would not again write. Mr. Lerew, when he called, perceived that she was very unhappy, and having drawn from her the cause of her grief, he assured her that there was but one way by which she could regain peace of mind, and insinuated that so bigoted a person as Captain Caulfield would in all probability discard her when he found that she was anxious to serve the Church.

"It will prove a great trial to you, my dear sister," he said ; "but for such you must be prepared ; and I would urge

you to seek in the duties of a religious
life that comfort and consolation you are
sure to find."

Several weeks more went by, during
which the vicar's influence over poor Clara
increased. No letter came from Harry
or from his father.

"He has discarded me," exclaimed
Clara. "I must seek for that peace and
rest where alone, Mr. Lerew assures me, I
can find it, or I shall die."

The very next day, accompanied by
Mr. Lerew and his wife, Clara set off to
the town of ——, in the neighbourhood
of which was situated St. Barbara's, as
the convent was called. It had originally
been a religious house, as the term is,
and was encircled by a high wall, which
enclosed the garden and outhouses. It
was a dark, red brick, sombre pile, and
the additions lately made to it had given

it a thoroughly conventual appearance.
The carriage drove under an archway
in front of the entrance, closed on the
outside. Mr. Lerew got out and tugged
at a large iron bell-pull, when a slide in
the door was pulled back, and the face of a
female, who narrowly scrutinized the visitors, appeared at the opening. Mr. Lerew
quickly explained their object; no further words were exchanged, and after
a short delay the bars and bolts were
withdrawn, and the door was opened
sufficiently to allow him and his wife and
Clara to pass through into a small hall,
where they were left standing, while the
portress by signs summoned two serving
Sisters dressed in dark blue, with brass
crosses at their necks, to bring in Clara's
luggage. The same person then beckoning the visitors to follow, led them into
a waiting-room on one side. All the

time she had kept her eyes fixed on the ground, not once looking at the vicar's countenance. Having by signs desired them to be seated on some antique-looking chairs, which with a table and writing materials were the sole furniture of the room, she retired. Poor Clara felt dreadfully oppressed, and very much inclined to beg that her trunks might be put back again into the carriage, as she wished to return home; but pride, not unmixed with fear of the remarks Mr. Lerew would make, prevented her. She sat with her hand on her sinking heart, wondering whether all the members of the sisterhood would be expected to keep a perpetual silence.

"This reminds me much of the convents I have visited in France and Belgium," observed Mr. Lerew, turning to his wife. "Our young friend will soon learn the rules of the house, and see how suitable they are, and calculated to advance the religious feelings."

He spoke in a low tone, as if afraid of disturbing the solemn silence which reigned in the building. Some time passed away, when the door slowly opened, and a lady habited in grey, with a large cross inlaid with ivory on her breast, glided into the room. She was of commanding figure, and, in spite of her unbecoming head-dress and the white band across her brow, she had evidently once been handsome. She smiled benignantly as she glanced at Mrs. Lerew and Clara, and advancing to the vicar, bowed gracefully to him, and taking his hand, raised it to her lips; then retiring without further noticing her other guests, sank into a seat.

."I have come with my wife to introduce a young friend who is desirous of commencing, and I trust continuing, the life of a *réligieuse,*" said Mr. Lerew; " and from my knowledge of your admirable sisterhood, I feel confident that she will here obtain all she desires."

The Lady Superior now turned a piercing glance on Clara, which made her involuntarily shrink and cast down her eyes on the ground. The former did not speak till she had finished her scrutiny; she then said slowly,—-

" If you truly desire to embrace our holy calling, you will be gladly received, understanding that you must conform to the rules of our order in all respects. You will in the first instance enter as a postulant for a short time, during which you will wear your secular habit; after which you will become a probationer, and then, as I trust, we shall receive you as a confirmed

Sister on your vowing obedience to the three fundamental rules of our order. Are you prepared to remain with us at once?"

"Certainly, certainly," exclaimed Mr. Lerew; "Miss Maynard has come with that especial object in view. He who puts his hand to the plough must not turn back, nor would she, I am sure, wish to do so."

"What I would urge upon you," said the Lady Superior, "is complete self-surrender, and strict observance of the rule of holy obedience; without that you cannot expect to enjoy spiritual life, nor can the affairs of the community be properly carried on."

"I will endeavour to the best of my power to observe the rules of the order," said Clara, in a trembling voice.

"Of course she will, of course," observed Mr. Lerew; "it will be her glory and pride to do so. Oh what a beneficent arrangement is that by which a poor frail woman or layman can, by opening his or her heart to the priest, obtain all the instruction or advice for which their souls yearn!"

"You will soon be accustomed to the quiet life we lead within these walls," observed the Lady Superior, turning to Clara, without noticing Mr. Lerew's remark; "and I will invite you now to accompany me, when I will make you known to the Deane, who will initiate you into the rules and observances to which you will at once conform ; and you may now bid farewell to your friends, for they will excuse me, as my official duties require my attention."

Clara rose, and put out her hand to take that of Mr. Lerew. Instead, he bade her kneel, and placing his hands

above her head, uttered a benediction.
She felt inclined to embrace Mrs. Lerew
—not that she had any great affection
for her, but it seemed as if Mrs. Lerew
was the only link between her and the
world she was leaving; at that moment,
however, the Lady Superior, taking her
hand, led her towards the door.

"May I request an interview with Dr.
Catton, should he be now living here?"
asked Mr. Lerew.

"Our spiritual adviser is at present in
residence," answered the Lady Superior,
"and I will mention your wish to see
him, should you be able to remain till he
is at leisure."

"Oh, certainly, certainly. I must not
hurry Dr. Catton; but as it is a matter
of much importance, I much wish to
consult him. I will wait his pleasure,"
said Mr. Lerew.

Without having shown any act of courtesy to Mrs. Lerew, the Lady Superior left the room, still holding fast to Clara's hand.

"Had I expected to be so treated, I should not have come," exclaimed Mrs Lerew, as the door closed. "If these are conventual manners, I hope that Clara may not adopt them. What caused the Lady Superior to act as she did?"

"If you insist on knowing, you must understand that she probably considers priests ought to be celibates, and therefore looks upon you in no favourable light," answered the vicar, with some acerbity in his tone.

Mrs. Lerew was about to retort, when the door opened, and the spiritual adviser of the establishment, Dr. Catton, entered. He was a small thin man, with sallow complexion, and that peculiar pucker about the mouth which seems a characteristic of those who hold his views. The two gentlemen were well known to each other.

"I am anxious, my dear Doctor, to obtain your further advice regarding my new female college," said Mr. Lerew, "as I hope in a short time it will be in a sufficient state of advancement to receive pupils."

"I would gladly afford you my assistance in so holy a work," answered Dr. Catton, "as I consider it will tend greatly to the advancement of the Church; but——" and he looked at Mrs. Lerew.

"She is discreet, and takes a deep interest in the institution," said the vicar.

Dr. Catton looked as if he considered women were better out of the way when any matter of importance was to be discussed. However, as the vicar did not tell his wife to retire, he entered into the subject, speaking more cautiously perhaps than he otherwise would have done. Mrs. Lerew sat on, her countenance expressing her dissatisfaction at the want of confidence the Doctor placed in her. The rules and regulations of the new college were discussed, as well as the means for obtaining the necessary funds.

"You will understand that the young lady who is about to enter into this institution has a considerable fortune at her disposal, with which I have every hope she will endow our college. It must be a point of honour between us that she does not bestow it on the convent, and I beg that you will impress that on the mind of the Lady Superior. You will remember that I induced her to come here for that important object, for she will not be of age for upwards of two years, and she might in the meantime, were she to remain in the world, change her mind and marry, and her property would be lost to the Church."

"Of course," said Dr. Catton, "I am equally interested with you in the college, which I look upon as the nursing mother of those who will do much to forward the great cause."

After some further conversation on the subject, Mr. and Mrs. Lerew took their departure, Dr. Catton again promising that Clara's fortune should be appropriated as her father confessor desired. Clara had, in the meantime, been introduced to the Mother Eldress, a pleasant, fair lady of about forty, who took her round the establishment. The chapel was first visited. Over the high altar stood the crucifix, with paintings of the Virgin Mary on one side, and that of St. John on the other, and on it were the usual candlesticks with large wax candles and vases of flowers; while the walls were adorned with other paintings illustrating the lives of various saints, in which monks and nuns frequently appeared. The Mother Eldress drew aside a curtain which hung across a small side-chapel, when Clara saw, with considerable astonishment, the figure of the Virgin, richly dressed, standing on a small altar with candles burning on it, and also vases of flowers, with which the whole of the chapel was decked. The Mother Eldress bowed and crossed herself.

"You should do as I do," she said, turning to Clara; "the Blessed Virgin demands our most devoted love and adoration; we can never do her honour enough."

"I thought," observed Clara, "that as Protestants we did not worship the Virgin."

"Let me entreat you, my child, never to utter that odious word Protestant," exclaimed the Mother Eldress. "We are Catholics of the Anglican Church; we do not worship the Virgin either; but we love to do her honour."

Clara was puzzled; but thought it better just then to ask no further questions. The refectory and other public rooms were next visited; they were neat and scrupulously clean, but were destitute of every article of luxury, or which might conduce to comfort—no sofas, no easy arm-chairs were found in them.

"You will now like to see the cells," said the Mother Eldress, as she led the way upstairs. Passing along a gallery, she opened a door, and exhibited a long narrow room containing a camp bedstead, covered by a white quilt, a small table and a chair, and in one corner a desk with a Bible and a few books of devotion on it, as also a lamp, and above it a picture of the crucifixion. It was lighted by a small, deep, oriel window, with a broad sill, on which were arranged some flower-pots, sweet-scented flowers growing in them. No carpet covered the floor; but it was brightly polished, as was all the woodwork in the room.

"Such will be your dormitory," observed the Mother Eldress.

"Is there no fireplace?" asked Clara.

"There are in some of the cells; but such are not allowed to novices," was the answer.

Clara, who had been accustomed to a fire in winter all her life, shuddered; for even now, in the height of summer, the room felt cold.

"I will now show you the rules," said the Mother Eldress, producing a book in manuscript. "No letters must be written or received by the Sisters of St. Barbara, and any presents that may be made must be given to the Mother Superior for the use of the community. Sisters are always, whether by night or day, to enter the chapel with all alacrity, and in a perfect spirit of recollection, in order to prepare their souls for prayer. No Sister must be absent from the chapel without leave, and all must recite the offices. You see how well our time is divided," continued the lady; "we rise at three a.m.; there are primer, meditation, etc., until seven, when we enjoy the Holy Communion. After this we have prayers and self-examination until nine, and from that hour till ten we work. At ten we dine, which is the first meal we partake of in the day. We then take an hour for recreation, and another till twelve for meditation. From one till four we work, when we attend vespers, and from half-past four to half-past five we take tea and listen to spiritual reading. From half-past five to six we have again recreation, from six to seven prayers, at which hour we retire for the night; but we rise for prayer during one hour of the night, and at midnight on Thursdays we rise to spend an additional hour in prayer. Thus, you see, every moment of the day is portioned out. During the hours of work we tend the sick and visit the dying; we also are employed in other good undertakings, and we hope before long to establish fresh ones. So you see, my dear, that we work out our own salvation, though those who have a vocation to a purely religious life can enter our contemplative order, and devote themselves entirely to prayer and meditation. You will be able to judge by-and-by to which you would wish to belong, though you will, of course, be guided by the advice of the Mother Superior."

"Alas!" said Clara, "I do not feel myself fitted for either at present; but I believe that I should prefer attempting to teach the young—at least, the very young, for I should never manage big boys and girls. I used to teach some of the cottagers' little children in our neighbourhood, till I had entirely to devote myself to my dying father."

"You will learn by experience," said the Mother Eldress. "I will mention your wish to the Mother Superior, and she will probably appoint you to the duty you select. She has great discernment, and will perceive for which you are best fitted."

Clara thought that she herself could judge best of what she could do. She expressed as much to the Mother Eldress, who smiled, and reminded her of the rule of obedience. Altogether, Clara was tolerably well contented with the prospect before her. She was afterwards introduced to a number of the Sisters during their hour of recreation ; but she could not help remarking that whenever one addressed another, a nun, who she was told was the Deane, instantly interfered, and reminded the speaker that private conversation was against the rule. She discovered that there were to be no private intimacies, and that any conversation must be general.

"Can I not associate with any one whom I like?" asked Clara afterwards of the Mother Eldress.

"It is against the rule," was the answer ; "private friendships would destroy the harmony which must exist in our sisterhood."

"But cannot I express my sorrow or anxiety to a sympathising friend?" asked Clara, ingenuously.

"Such must be poured into the ear alone of the Mother Superior or of your father confessor," said the Mother Eldress in a stern tone; "discipline could not be otherwise maintained."

Clara felt unusually hungry at tea-time, as she had had but a slight luncheon; but as it was Friday—dry bread alone was allowed during the meal. One of the Eldresses read an allegorical work, the meaning of which Clara did not exactly comprehend, and from it therefore she did not gain much spiritual advantage. Another half-hour was spent in conversation, which was anything but spiritual, and then the nuns adjourned to the chapel, where they joined in reciting prayers, the same being repeated over and over again ; and at seven they retired to their cells. Clara, unaccustomed to go to bed at so early an hour, could not sleep : the past would recur to her. Against all rule she thought of Harry and the way she had treated him ; then she remembered all must be given up for the sake of following Christ—but was she following Him by entering a convent? The conflict was severe ; she burst into tears, and sobbed as if her heart would break. Hour after hour went by, sleep refusing to visit her eyelids, till, long after midnight, thoroughly worn out, she sobbed herself into forgetfulness.

The convent clock was striking three when a Sister entered her cell and summoned her to rise and repair to the chapel. Hastily dressing, she followed her conductress, who had remained to assist her. She there found all the nuns assembled, and for four hours they remained repeating prayers and chanting alternately, till Dr. Catton entered, and after going through a service, administered the Holy Communion, giving the wafer instead of bread, and wine mixed with water. Faint and weary, for nearly two hours more Clara remained, while the nuns repeated the prayers, or sat silent, engaged in self-examination. Some of them who had undertaken the duty of teachers then went into the schoolroom, where some fifty children were assembled. Clara begged leave to accompany them, and gladly took charge of three or four of the youngest, though by this time she felt so exhausted that she could with difficulty speak. The school over, the nuns hurried to the refectory, where a frugal dinner was placed on the table by the serving Sisters. In silence the nuns took their places ; in silence they ate the portions served to them. Clara, sick from hunger, had the greatest difficulty in swallowing the coarse and unpalatable food. It notwithstanding restored her strength, and she went through her duties in the schoolroom with rather more spirit than in the morning.

The following day was passed much as the first. Clara saw but little of the Mother Superior, who kept herself much aloof from the community, in her own apartments, which were furnished very differently to those of the nuns.

Several weeks passed by. Though Clara got accustomed to the ways of the establishment, and strictly followed the rules, she did not find herself more at home than at first, nor was she at all more intimate with the Sisters ; yet, girl as she was, she possessed an indomitable spirit.

Although the false religious fervour which had induced her to consent to enter a nunnery had vanished, she was determined not to give in on account of the disagreeables she experienced. Her aunt Sarah had promised to write to her, and she herself had written several times; but she received no letters, and dared not ask whether any had come for her. She remembered that till she wrote her aunt would not know her address, unless Mr. Lerew had given it.

The short time that it was necessary to remain as a postulant had expired, and in a formal service in the chapel she was received as a probationer, and assumed the dress of the order. Scarcely a day had passed before she found herself exposed to annoyances which she had not hitherto experienced. During the hours of recreation the Deane, whose duty it was to keep the Sisters in order, was continually rebuking her for some transgression of rules, either for laughing or talking too much, or addressing a Sister in a voice which the rest could not hear; and she had to undergo in consequence all sorts of penalties. She submitted, as she considered that she was in duty bound to do, though she felt that they were far severer than the faults demanded. She could discover none of the religious fervour which she had expected to find among the Sisters, or of love or sympathy. Her own spirit, though not broken, was kept under a thraldom, against which her judgment rebelled. It appeared to her that the system was far better adapted to keep in subjection a household of people out of their minds than a collection of ladies in their right senses, who wished to serve God and do their duty to their

fellow-creatures. No Sister was allowed
to visit another in her cell, and sometimes
for days and weeks together Clara did
not see some of the Sisters whom she
had met on her first arrival. Where
they had gone, or what they were about,
she could not learn. Little attention was
paid to those who were ill, and no
sympathy was expressed. A young
Sister who had been sent out on a begging expedition for the order, and had
to trudge through the wet day after day,
caught cold, and was obliged to return.
She grew pale and thin, and the ominous
red spot appeared on her cheek. She
coughed incessantly, but still went
through her duties. At night she suffered
most; and to prevent the sound from disturbing others, she was ordered to move
to a distant cell, without a stove by which
it could be warmed. Clara determined,

against the rules, to speak to her, and offered to come and sit by her; but she shook her head, replying, " It must not be —you are wrong ;" at the same time the countenance of the dying girl expressed her gratitude. Clara's infraction of the rules being discovered, she was ordered to remain during the hours of recreation in solitude in her own cell.

The invalid Sister had crawled into the chapel one morning, and contrived with tottering steps to find her way back to her cell. The next morning she did not appear at matins, and when the Eldress went to see what had become of her, she was found stretched on her bed, dead, her pillow and sheets stained with blood, which had flowed from her mouth. She was not the only one whose life was thus sacrificed during Clara's novitiate.

One day there was great commotion in

the convent; the father of a novice had appeared at the gate, armed with legal powers which the Lady Superior dared not disobey, insisting on taking away his daughter. The young lady was told that she might go, with a warning that by so doing she was risking her soul's welfare. She had to take her departure in the dress of the order, leaving behind every article she had brought in, her own clothes having been sold for the benefit of the community. The dreadful fate to which she was doomed, and the fearful crime of her father, were daily expatiated on.

Some months passed by, when her father died, and Dr. Catton immediately wrote, urging her to return, and stating that if she did not do so, he could no longer remain her spiritual director, and thus she would lose the benefit of absolution. Letter after letter was sent to the same effect, and at length the poor girl, terrified by the consequences to which, as she supposed, her conduct had exposed her, came back to the convent. She was received in a stern manner by the Mother Superior, in the presence of the community, being told that it was through love for her soul that she had been readmitted; but that she must for a whole year hold no intercourse with the other novices, and must remain in solitude during the time allowed each day for recreation; while she was pointed to as a warning to the rest. This discipline preyed greatly on her mind, and Clara, whose cell was next to hers, heard her weeping night after night. When she appeared in public, she hung down her head, and scarcely tasted any of the meagre fare placed before her; taught to suppose that fasting was a virtue, or else weary of the life she was doomed to lead, she was starving herself to death.

Notwithstanding all the vigilance exercised, the novices did contrive at times to hold communication with each other, and one young girl, who looked very sad, and was evidently dangerously ill, confessed to Clara that she had escaped from her home to join the convent against the express wishes of her father, whom notwithstanding she asserted that she loved dearly. She had ever been among the most obedient to the commands of the Lady Superior, and the strictest in complying with the rules of the order. Her illness increased ; she at last received the news of the death of that parent whose wishes she had disobeyed. The thought that her disobedience had deeply grieved him whom she was bound to love preyed on her mind, and tended much to aggravate her disease; the arguments brought forward by the Lady Superior, and Mother Eldress, and her father confessor, that God had the first çlaims on her, failed to assuage her sorrow, or to persuade her that she had acted rightly. Clara, observing that she looked more than usually ill when they parted in the evening, could not refrain from going into her cell. She found her on her bed, gasping for breath.

"Thank you for coming," whispered the poor girl; "it would have been hard to die all alone. My poor father! my poor father!" she murmured; "would that I could have been with him!"

She could utter no more. Clara, to her horror, while bending over her, found that the poor sufferer had breathed her last. She hurried to the apartment of the Mother Eldress, who came somewhat agitated to the dead Sister's cell; but instead of expressing any grief at the occurrence, she sternly rebuked Clara for breaking the rules, and ordered her back to her own cell. The Sisters assembled at the usual hour in the chapel; but not a word was said of the occurrence of the night. The nun was buried with ceremonies resembling those of Rome, and things went on as usual.

The Mother Eldress, who was looked upon as a very saintly person, was at length taken ill, and Clara was ordered to attend on her. The medical adviser of the sisterhood was sent for, and prescribed certain remedies which Clara had to administer. A small spoon had been provided for giving some powders in preserve; Clara used it daily for some time, till the Mother Eldress recovered, when the Lady Superior took possession of it. She had been in the habit of late of sending for Clara to impart religious instruction, which, she observed, she much required ; not failing at times, however, to lecture her severely. The day after the Mother Eldress had recovered from her illness the Lady Superior addressed Clara in a more serious tone even than usual.

"You will observe, my daughter," she said, "that miracles have not ceased ; but that some communions, alas! have not faith to perceive them. We, holding the Catholic doctrine in its purity, have been more favoured. Let me ask of what metal you conceive that the spoon with which you used to administer the medicine to our beloved Mother Eldress is composed."

"It was, I should say, of silver, or rather plated," answered Clara.

"Originally it might have been; but see here, it is turned to gold," answered the Lady Superior, producing the spoon, which had now evidently a yellow tinge.

"I observed that before," said Clara, "and believed that it was produced by the nature of the medicine."

"Oh, hard of heart, and slow to believe!" exclaimed the Lady Superior; "can you not now perceive that it is gold, pure gold? By what other than by miraculous power could this change have been wrought? Let the glorious fact be known among the Sisters, and all who desire may come and witness it."

Clara was not convinced; she went away wondering whether the Lady Superior was deceived herself, or desired to deceive others. Many of the nuns were highly delighted at hearing of the miracle, which tended so much to prove that their establishment was under the especial protection of Heaven. The Mother Eldress crossed her hands on her bosom, while she meekly bowed her head, and expressed her gratitude that she should have been so remarkably favoured. It was evident, however, to Clara, that some of the Sisters were sceptical on the subject.

Clara found the life she was doomed to lead more and more irksome; but when she compared it with that of the Sisters who belonged to the order of the Sacred Heart, the true nuns, who were even more strictly enclosed (as the term is) than were she and her associates, she felt that she had no right to complain. The nuns of the Sacred Heart, or as they were frequently called, of the order of the Love of Jesus, were supposed to spend their time in perpetual prayer for the living or the dead. The whole of the twenty-four hours, Clara learned, are divided into what are denominated watches; the night watches being kept by the nuns in the following manner. The Sisters retire at seven o'clock, with the exception of one who remains watching till eight. She then summons another Sister, who rises and watches till nine, the latter again summoning a fresh watcher, and thus they continue till three o'clock, when all assemble in the chapel for matins. They also join in prayer seven times in the day, at fixed periods, though they may be separated. To the order of the Love of Jesus are attached companions who may mix in the world, and whose real duties are to obtain proselytes. They are expected to join in prayer at stated hours, wherever they may be, and on every Thursday night, from midnight till one o'clock, the companions unite in prayer. The Lady Superior in one of her more confidential moods invited Clara to join the order.

"My dear child," she observed, "it is a glorious thing to be thus constantly engaged in prayer when you may; in every service and homage you render, call to your aid the choirs of angelic spirits, and unite yourself to them in spiritual companionship, in order that they may supply your deficiencies."

Clara had never before heard that it was necessary to obtain the aid of angels for offering up prayer to God, and was somewhat startled at the novelty of the notion; but she knew perfectly well that it would not do to state her objections to so determined a person as her spiritual mother. She did not, either, feel inclined to become one of the order of the Sacred Heart, not having formed the very highest opinion of the nuns belonging to it whom she had met. They appeared to her generally weak-minded enthusiasts, and she still retained a belief that God is best served by those who, in imitation of our blessed Lord and Master, engage in the duties of active benevolence. On her declining, therefore, the Lady Superior dismissed her in a stern manner, reminding her that those who put their hands to the plough, and look back, are not worthy of the kingdom of heaven.

Clara, without uttering a word, left the room, and hoped to devote herself with more zeal than ever to the duties she had actually undertaken. With this feeling, she repaired at the appointed hour to the school-room, where she took her class of children. They were, as it happened, inclined to be less attentive and more unruly than was their wont; some of them had only lately been induced to attend the school, and were unaccustomed to the rules and regulations. A biggish boy was trying to see how far he could proceed in impudence and lead on the others, when Clara, finding that appealing to him was useless, gave him a box on the ear. The Deane, at that moment entering, observed the act.

" Sister Clare," she exclaimed, " I must take your class ; retire to your cell."

Clara, not believing that she had done anything wrong, got up and obeyed the order. Had she remained, she would have seen that the Deane's temper was tried as much as hers had been. On reaching her cell she sat down, wondering whether any further notice would be taken of her conduct. Scarcely had the convent clock announced that school was over, than the Deane appeared, and ordered her to go to the Lady Superior. She was met with a frowning brow.

"You have given way to temper—you require humbling, my daughter," exclaimed the lady; "I must take means to lower that proud and haughty spirit of yours. Return to your cell, and wait till the Mother Eldress comes for you."

Clara bowed and obeyed. After she had waited for some minutes, the Mother Eldress appeared, and taking her hand, led her along the gallery to an empty room, which, not having been used for many months, the floor was covered with dust.

"Enter there,' she said, "and show your contrition by kneeling on your knees, and licking with your tongue the form of the Blessed Cross on the ground."

Clara stood aghast.

"Are you serious?" she asked

"It is the command of the Lady

Superior, and you are bound by your vow of obedience to obey her orders—break them at the peril of your soul, Sister Clare," was the answer. "Go in, and let me be able to report that you have exhibited sorrow for your fault by performing the penance which your spiritual superior in her wisdom has thought fit to inflict."

No sooner had Clara entered the room than the door was locked on her. Degraded and abased in her own eyes, all her moral feelings revolting against the abominable indignity imposed on her, yet the threat which had been uttered made her tremble She had vowed implicit obedience. With loathing at her heart, with a feeling too bitter to allow her tears to flow, she performed the debasing act, forgetting that the marks she was thus making on the ground was the accepted symbol of the Christian faith.

Still, the words occurred to her, "Rend your hearts, and not your garments, and turn unto the Lord your God." Could the God of all love and mercy and gentleness be pleased by such an act? It might degrade her in her own sight; but could it make her heart more truly humble, more anxious to serve Him who said, "Come unto me, all ye that labour and are heavy laden, and I will give you rest"?

Clara had a Bible in her pocket. To calm her agitation, she read a portion, earnestly praying for instruction. The words which brought conviction to Luther met her sight. Light beamed on her troubled mind. The mists which the vicar's sophistries had gathered round her rolled away. "From henceforth I will look to Jesus alone, to the teaching of His Word, the guidance of His Holy Spirit," she exclaimed. Clara was free.

Chapter V.

AT length General Caulfield, having arranged the affairs of his brother who had died, returned to Luton. He had been made very anxious and unhappy by the letters he received from Harry, who expressed his astonishment at not hearing from Clara. The general, supposing that she was still at home, and fearing that she must be ill, immediately on his arrival set off to pay her a visit.

"Miss Maynard is away; Miss Pemberton is at home, sir," said the servant who opened the door.

Miss Pemberton received him in a stiff

and freezing manner. He immediately enquired for Clara.

"My niece has, for some time, left home, and has not communicated her address to me, nor has she thought fit to write, so that I am in ignorance of where she is," was the unsatisfactory answer.

"That is most extraordinary," cried the general; "can you not give me any clue by which I may discover her?"

"I conclude, as she has not informed me of her abode, that she does not wish it to be known," answered Miss Pemberton, evasively.

"Though you do not know where your niece is, is Mr. Lerew, or is her father's old friend, Mr. Lennard, acquainted with her present address?" asked the general.

"I should think that she would have informed me rather than any one else," replied Miss Pemberton; and the general at length, finding that he could get no information out of the lady, took his leave.

"I will try, at all events, to ascertain what either Lennard or Lerew know," said the general to himself, as he drove off. Though he suspected that the vicar knew something about the matter, he decided first to call on Mr. Lennard. He believed him to be an honest man, but he had no great opinion of his sense. Mr. Lennard was at home; he received the general in a kindly way. The latter observed that his manner was unusually subdued. Without loss of time, the general mentioned Miss Maynard, and expressed his regret at not finding her at home.

"Can you tell me where she has gone to?" he asked, "for her aunt declares that she does not know, though it was evident from her manner that she is not anxious about her."

"I regret to say that I know no more than you do," answered Mr. Lennard. "I had been for some time absent, and on my return I was greatly surprised to find that she had left Luton ; and when I enquired of the Lerews, they told me that she had resolved to devote herself to works of charity, and was about to enter a sisterhood, but in what neighbourhood they did not inform me."

"In other words, that she is about to become a nun, to discard my poor son, and to give up her property, as soon as she has the power of disposing of it, to the safe keeping of one of those Romish communities," exclaimed the general, with more vehemence than he was accustomed to exhibit ; "what do you say to that, Mr. Lennard ?"

"I don't suppose that Miss Maynard purposes entering a Romish convent ; her

intention, I conclude, is to join a sisterhood of the Anglican Church," said Mr.
Lennard.

" The Church of England, of which I
suppose you speak, recognises no such
institutions," replied the general; " they
are contrary to the spirit of the Reformation. Unhappy will it be for our country
if they ever gain ground."

"I had been inclined to suppose that
they would prove a great advantage, by
enabling ladies to unite together and work
under a good system in visiting the sick
and poor, and in the instruction of the
children, and in other beneficent labours;
and I have, when requested, subscribed
towards their support," remarked Mr.
Lennard.

" I do not insist that ladies should not
thus employ themselves," observed the
general; "but my objection is to the mode

in which they unite themselves in the so-called religious system under which they are placed. They may, in most instances, serve God far better by staying at home and doing their duty in their families, instead of assuming the dress and imitating the customs of the nuns of the middle ages."

"I do not look at the subject in that light," observed Mr. Lennard, "and I know that it must be a hard matter for some young ladies to be religious at home, where the rest of the family are worldly-minded."

"Much more reason for them to stay at home and endeavour to improve the tone of the rest of the household," answered the general. "Those who know what human nature is should see that with whatever good intentions these sisterhoods are begun, they must in the end lead to much that is objectionable. If Miss Maynard has joined one of them, I must endeavour to find the means of getting her out, or of ascertaining if she was induced to join it, and remains of her own free will. I fear that Lerew will not afford me any assistance, as from his Romish tendencies he will probably consider them admirable institutions, and would think that he had done a laudable act in inducing Clara to enter one. I must now wish you good-bye. I hope that you have good accounts of your young daughter Mary, and your son at Oxford."

Mr. Lennard shook his head. " I received a letter to-day from my little girl, saying that she was very ill, and begging me to come and take her home ; but as the mistress did not write, I do not suppose that her illness is serious. However, I intend to go to-morrow to Mary, and ascertain how she is, and I trust that I shall not be obliged to take her away from school."

The general considered whether he should call on Mr. Lerew ; but he first bethought himself of paying a visit to a lawyer in the neighbouring town, with whom he was well acquainted, and who had been a friend of Captain Maynard's. He was also an earnest religious man, and strongly opposed to ritualism. The general was not a person to let the grass grow under his feet. He was driving rapidly along, when he met Lieutenant Sims, who made a sign to him to stop. The general did so, and invited the lieutenant to accompany him into the town.

"With all my heart, for I want to have a talk with you, general," answered the lieutenant, springing in. "I have long been wishing for your return. We've had some extraordinary goings on in this place. What has concerned me most is the disappearance of my old friend's daughter, in whom you, I know, take a deep interest. All I know is that she went away with the vicar and his wife, and it is my belief that they had an object in spiriting her off; but whether to shut her up in a Romish or Ritualist convent is more than I can say. I don't think there is much to choose between them; the vicar might select the Ritualist, or the Anglican, as he would call it, as he, though a Papist at heart, would prefer keeping his living, while his lady would recommend the former; for it is said, and I believe it to be a fact, that she herself has turned Romanist, with her dear friend Lady Bygrave. Haven't you heard that both Sir Reginald and her ladyship were received last week into the bosom of the Church of Rome, as the expression runs ?"

" Is it possible ! " exclaimed the general; "but I ought not to be surprised when I saw the characters they admitted into their house. I thought that French abbé and Father Lascelles had some other object in view than the establishment of a colony ; but perhaps you have been mis-informed."

" I tell you, general, I haven't a doubt about the matter," answered Mr. Sims. " They and Mrs. Lerew attended the Romish church together, and I am told had been baptized with all ceremony a few days before. I know that two or three priests have been staying at the Hall ever since, and Mrs. Lerew goes there regularly. They are about to have a chapel built in their grounds, and an architect came down from London about it ; and in the meantime they have got a room fitted up in the house. What surprises me is that the vicar should allow his wife to turn ; but that she has done so seems probable, for she was not at church last Sunday. Should Lerew object to his wife's perversion, he has only himself to thank for it ; he has led her up to the door as carefully as a man could do, and cannot be surprised at her going inside. Of course she thinks it safer to join what she has been taught to look upon as the true church, and has therefore honestly gone over to it ; while whatever he may think, putting honesty and honour aside, he considers that it is more to his advantage to retain his living, and lead others in the way he has led his wife."

"I suspect that you are right," observed

the general; "too many have set him the example. He, like them, has been trained in the school of the Jesuits, who are fully persuaded that evil may be done that good may come of it, and banish from their minds the principles which guide honest men, and which they themselves would advocate in the ordinary affairs of life. I can only wish that, unless Mr. Lerew's mind is enlightened, he would go over himself; as I am afraid, while he remains in the Church of England, he may lead others in the same direction."

"Not much fear of that," observed the lieutenant; "except a few silly young people of the better classes, and the poor, who look out for the loaves and fishes in the shape of coals and blankets and other creature comforts, I don't think many are influenced by him. He is more likely to empty his church, and to fill the Dissenting chapels."

"*Still*," said the general, "he sows broadcast the germs of Romanism through the doctrines he preaches, while he accustoms people to the sight of the ceremonies and paraphernalia of Rome, keeping them in ignorance at the same time of the simple truths of the Gospel, at the bidding of those whose commands he obeys; for he and his ritualistic brethren are but instruments in the hands of more cunning men than themselves. I have little doubt that he was carefully educated at the university for the part he is now playing, though he then had no idea of the designs of his tutor. People laugh at the notion that a Jesuit plot has long existed in England for the subversion of Protestantism; but I have evidence, which receives daily corroboration, that Jesuits

in disguise matriculated at the universities
for the express purpose of perverting the
minds of all whom they could bring
under their influence. The pupils in
numberless instances went over to Rome,
while the tutors remained nominally in
the Church of England, for the sake
of trapping others. The scheme has
succeeded, and has since been greatly
enlarged ; the Jesuits have now agents
in every shape—some as incumbents of
parishes, as lay supporters, men and
women, guilds and sisterhoods ; they have
encouraged works of charity, schools,
hospitals, refuges for the fallen and
destitute, *crêches*, mothers' meetings, and
other institutions, all excellent in themselves, knowing how much such would forward their object. Of that object, those
who take part in them are, I am ready
to believe, in many instances utterly igno-

rant; they are influenced by the desire to obey the commands of Christ, and to make themselves useful to their fellow-creatures, though the idea that they are thereby meriting heaven, and what they call working out their own salvation, underlies all they do, as they misinterpret the passage. They ignore the glorious truth that through simple faith in the atoning blood of Christ salvation is gained— that it is their own, and that the right motive of action must be through love and obedience to Him who has already saved them. All the forms and ceremonies in which they indulge are but will-worship, tending to obscure their view of Him, and to destroy their spiritual life."

"General," said the lieutenant, "I have seen a good deal of Roman Catholic countries, where the priests have full sway, and I am very sure that the system these Ritualists have introduced is tending in the same direction. I know from experience that true religion makes a man all that can be expected of him. We had a dozen or more such men on board the last ship in which I served, and they were out and out the best men we had; they could be trusted on all occasions; and if any dangerous work had to be done, they were the first to volunteer. They were Dissenters of some sort, I believe, and were not in favour with our ritualistic chaplain, who had his followers both among officers and men. I can't say much about those officers, and as to the men who pretended to agree with him, they were the most sneaking rascals in the ship. He tried to bring me over to his way of thinking, but my eyes were opened. 'No, no,' I answered; 'if the ship was going down, and you had to take your chance in one of the boats, which would you choose, the one manned by those fellows you anathematize, or with the men you call obedient sons of the Church?' He couldn't answer; but one day, he being left on shore, the heretics, as he called them, brought him off through a heavy surf, when no other men would venture. So you see, thanks to our chaplain, when I found the new vicar working changes in the church, I knew pretty well what he was about."

The general found Mr. Franklin, his solicitor, at home.

"I am very glad you have come, general," said the latter. "Miss Maynard, as you are probably aware, has been induced to leave home, or, rather, has been entrapped by one of those conventual establishments, to which she will in due course, when she has the power, be persuaded to give up her property. Our business must be to get her out of their hands before that time arrives ; and yours, general, more especially to point out to her the errors of the system which has thrown its glamour over her ; for, if I understand rightly, she has sacrificed an excellent and satisfactory marriage, as well as the independence and comforts of home. It was not for a considerable time that I discovered her absence from Luton, when her aunt (who, no disrespect to the lady, I consider it a misfortune was left one of her guardians) positively declared that she did not know where she had gone. I, however, took steps to find out, and lately ascertained that she is an inmate of St. Barbara's, near Staughton, to which place I discovered that she drove

on leaving the railway, in company with
Mr. and Mrs. Lerew. Convinced that
Miss Pemberton was not likely to render
any willing assistance, I awaited your
return to take legal measures to obtain
her release. Our first difficulty will be to
communicate with her, for the nuns are
allowed to receive no letters till they are
first seen by the Lady Superior. It
would be as well first to ascertain whether
the young lady desires of her own free
will to leave the convent; she has had
some experience of it, and may by this
time perhaps have repented of the step
she has taken. My belief is that she has
been deceived and cajoled. I know well
of what those Ritualists are capable, influenced by what they believe the best of
motives, and I strongly suspect that there
is some misunderstanding between her
and your son, brought about, I say with-

out hesitation, by their means. Either
her letters have not been forwarded to
him, or his have not been received by her
—perhaps the entire correspondence has
been intercepted—I will not go farther
than that. I say this as I wish to plead
for your ward, at whose conduct you
naturally feel deeply grieved."

"Poor girl! notwithstanding all the
pain and suffering she has caused my
son, I am not angry with her," said the
general; "my indignation is directed
against the system and persons by whom
she has been deceived. I suspect as you
do with regard to the correspondence
between her and my son, for I am very
sure she would not have given him up
without assigning any reason, or answer-
ing his letters."

"Our first object must be to open a free
communication with her; letters sent in

the ordinary way are sure to be read by the Lady Superior, and the answers dictated by her, so that we shall not be wiser than at first," remarked Mr. Franklin.

"I must try that simple plan, however, and if it fails, resort to stronger measures," observed the general. "I will go to Staughton myself, and write to say that, as her guardian, I wish to have a private interview with her on a matter of importance, and to beg that I may be allowed to call on her at the convent, or that she will come and see me at my hotel."

"I am afraid that means would be taken to prevent her from seeing you alone," observed Mr. Franklin.

"What course do you then advise?" asked the general.

"We must take legal proceedings, and they are very certain to have their due effect, as the Lady Superior would be exceedingly loth to have the internal arrangements of her convent made public, and she is well aware that if she resists she will run the risk of that being the case. I have already had something to do with her ladyship, as well as with two or three other convents, and I know how jealous the managers are that the secrets of their prison-houses should be revealed. Their aim is to prove they have nothing to conceal, and that all is open as noon-day; but the moment troublesome questions are asked, they exhibit a reticence as to their rules and practices which shows how conscious they are that outsiders will object to them."

Before the general took his leave, it was arranged between him and Mr. Franklin that they should go over together to Epsworth, and act according to circumstances.

As he drove home he expressed a hope to the honest lieutenant that he might be the means of emancipating Miss Maynard from her present thraldom.

"She has too much sense and right feeling not to be open to conviction," answered Mr. Sims ; "what she wants is to be freed from the evil influences to which she has of late been exposed, and to have the simple truth placed before her ; only don't let her meet her aunt or Mr. Lerew till she has thoroughly got rid of all her erroneous notions, and understands the simple gospel as you well know how to put it."

"You may depend on my following your advice," said the general.

On reaching home, the general found a note from Mr. Lennard. He wrote in great distress of mind. He had received a letter from a friend at Oxford, telling him that his son had left the university in company with a Romish priest, and had declared his intention of seeking admission into the Church of Rome. Mr. Lennard was anxious, if possible, to find out his son, and prevent him from taking the fatal step, at the same time that he wished to be with his poor little girl at Cheltenham.

" I am afraid," he continued, " that the tutor under whom I placed my boy, by Mr. Lerew's advice, has had much to do with it. I now hear that three or four of his previous pupils have become Romanists, and others, by all accounts, are likely to go over. I object to my son's becoming a Romanist, though I consider that the Church of Rome is the mother of all Churches, and has the advantage of antiquity on her side."

" The mother of all abominations!" exclaimed the general to himself. "I must endeavour to set my friend right on that subject, if he holds that fundamental error."

The general was a man of action. After taking a hurried meal, he drove on to the house of Mr. Lennard. His journey to Cheltenham had been delayed, and he was now hesitating whether first to go in search of his son or to proceed there immediately. The thought at once struck the general that should he succeed in getting Clara out of the convent, he might go on to Cheltenham with her, and that if Mary was fit to be removed from the school, it would give Clara occupation to nurse her friend.

"I shall indeed be most grateful to you," said Mr. Lennard, with the tears in his eyes; "I was sorely perplexed what to do, and I specially wish that Mary should not remain longer at the school than can be helped, as from her letter it is evident that she is not only ill, but very miserable there.

"You must give me your written authority, and I will act upon it," said the general. This was done. "Now, my friend," he continued, "I wish to speak to you on the remark made in your letter, in which you say that you consider the Church of Rome the mother of all Churches, and that it has the advantage of antiquity. You evidently go first on the assumption that our Lord instituted a visible Church on earth, and that that Church, though corrupted, is the Church of Rome. Now I wish to draw your attention to the origin of that wonderful establishment which has for so long exerted a baneful influence over a large portion of the human race.

For three centuries true Christians, though becoming less and less pure in their doctrine and form of worship, existed in Rome as a despised and subordinate class, the purity of their faith gradually decreasing as their numbers, wealth, and influence increased. At length the Emperor Constantine professed himself to be a Christian, which he did for the sake of obtaining the assistance of the Christians against his rival Licinius, who was supported by the idolaters. Constantine being victorious, and Licinius slain, the idolaters saw that they could no longer hope to be predominant. There existed in Rome from the days of Numa a college, or curia, the members of which, called pontiffs, had the entire management of all matters connected with religion. The post of head pontiff, or Pontifex Maximus, had been assumed by Julius Cæsar and his successors. They had probably no real belief in the idolatrous system they supported; such secret faith as they had was centred in Astarte, the divinity of the ancient Babylonians, whose worship had been introduced at an early period into Etruria, as it had been previously into Egypt and Greece. They were, in reality, the priests of Astarte, and from them we derive our festival of Christmas, our Lady Day, and many other festivals with Christian names. It had been their principle from the first to admit any gods who had become popular, and thus were added in rapid succession the numberless gods and goddesses of the heathen mythology. At length Jesus of Nazareth was added to their pantheon. These pontiffs, on perceiving that Christianity, patronized by the Emperor, was likely to gain the day, saw that to maintain their power they must themselves pretend to belong to the new faith. This they did, and one of their number soon managed to get himself chosen the Bishop of Rome, while the other pontiffs by an easy transition formed the College of Cardinals. The title of Pontifex Maximus, being held by the Emperor, was not assumed by the bishop of Rome till the Emperor Gratian in 376 refused any longer to be addressed by that title. Having banished some of the grosser practices of idolatry, they introduced the remainder under different names, so that the pagans might readily conform to the new worship. The apostles took the place of the various gods, and the martyrs those of the inferior divinities ; above them all was raised Astarte, who, now named Mary the Mother of God and Queen of Heaven, became the chief object of adoration. In truth, the established worship at Rome remained as truly idolatrous as it had ever been, while the great aim of the pontiffs was to increase their power, amass wealth, and strengthen their position. From that period they acted, as might have been expected, in direct opposition to all the principles of Christianity. Bloody struggles often took place between rivals aiming at the pontificate, while they endeavoured to destroy all those who refused to obey them. It was not till a somewhat later period, when the head pontiff set up a claim of superiority above all other bishops, that, to strengthen it, it was asserted that he was in direct apostolic succession from the apostle Peter, the pontiff who first made it being ignorant, probably, that the Christian Church at Rome was founded exclusively by Paul, and that the apostle Peter never was at Rome, he having been all his life employed in founding churches in the East. 'By their fruits ye shall know them;' and we have only to reflect on the lives of the popes, many of them monsters of atrocity, and the fearful acts of persecution which they encouraged and authorized, to be convinced that paganism, the invention of Satan, had usurped the name of Christianity, and that the Romish Church, as it is called, instead of being the mother of all Churches, is truly the Babylon of the Apocalypse; yet this is the system which ministers of the Church of England are endeavouring to introduce into our country, with its idolatrous rites and dogmas, and which you and many excellent men like yourself look at with a lenient eye, instead of regarding it with the abhorrence it deserves."

"My dear friend," said Mr. Lennard, greatly astonished, "I certainly had never regarded the Church of Rome in that light; I looked upon it as the ancient Church, corrupted in the course of ages."

" It has no true claim to be a Christian Church at all," said the general; "it is like the cuckoo, which, hatched in the nest of the hedge-warbler, by degrees forces out the other fledglings, and usurps their place. So did paganism treat Christianity; although, fostered by God, the latter was enabled to exist, persecuted and oppressed as it was, and still to exert a benign influence in the world. On examining the tenets of many who are called heretics, we find that it was not the creed they held, but the opposition they offered to the Romish system, which was their crime, and brought down persecution on their heads. When we read of the horrible cruelties practised on the Waldenses and Albigenses, the followers of Huss in Bohemia, the true Protestants of all ages down to the time of Luther, the detestable system of the Inquisition, the treatment of the inhabitants of the Netherlands by Alva and the Spaniards, when whole hecatombs of victims were put to death at the instigation of the pope and his cardinals, the destruction of thousands and tens of thousands of Huguenots in France, the martyrdoms of the noble Protestants of Spain, the massacre of St. Bartholomew, and the fires of Smithfield—all these diabolical acts performed with the concurrence and approval of the papal power—can we for a moment hesitate to believe that that power owes its origin, not to the Divine Head of the Church, but to that spirit of evil, Satan, the deadly foe of the human race? Can any system founded on it, however much reformed it may appear, fail to partake of the evil inherent in the original itself. It is from not seeing this that so many are led to embrace the errors—I would rather say the abominations—of Rome; while others are taught to look at them with lenient eyes, and to believe that the system itself is capable of reformation. Before true and simple faith can be established throughout the world the whole must be overthrown and hurled into the depths of the sea, as completely as have been the idols and idolatrous practices of the inhabitants of the South Sea Islands, where Christianity has been established."

Mr. Lennard leant his head on his hand. "I must think deeply of what you say; you put the whole matter in a new light to me. I have had no affection for Rome; still, I have always regarded her as a Church founded on the apostles and prophets."

"Yet which virtually forbids its followers to study those prophets and apostles," remarked the general. But what I want you to do is to look into the subject for yourself. I have merely given you a hint for your guidance; by referring carefully to the Scriptures, you will find more and more light thrown on it, till you must be convinced that the view I have taken is the correct one; and would that every clergyman and layman in England might do the same! these ritualistic practices would then soon be banished from the land."

Never in his life had poor Mr. Lennard been so perplexed and troubled. He was invited to reconsider opinions which he had held, in a somewhat lax fashion it may be granted, all his life. He had to search for his son, and prevent him if possible from becoming a slave to the system he had just heard so strongly denounced, and he was painfully anxious about the health of his dear little Mary. While he was still in this unhappy state of mind, the general left him to return home. The next morning they both set off to their respective destinations, the general to Epsworth, having called for Mr. Franklin on his way, and Mr. Lennard to London.

On reaching Epsworth, the general wrote a note to Clara, saying that as her guardian it was necessary for him to see her at once, and that he would either pay her a visit at the convent, or would request her to come to his hotel. After waiting for some time, he received a note in a strange handwriting; it was from a lady, who signed herself Sister Agatha. She stated that she wrote by the command of the Lady Superior, who was at present unwell, but would, on her recovery, reply to the letter General Caulfield had addressed to Sister Clare, or, as she was called in the world, Miss Clara Maynard.

"We must give her ladyship a taste of the law," said Mr. Franklin; "she fancies that she can play the same game with us which she has successfully employed with others. You shall write a note, stating that your legal adviser, Mr. Franklin, is with you; address it to the Lady Superior, and say that you insist on seeing Miss Maynard at once."

As soon as the letter was despatched, Mr. Franklin, observing that he had some business to transact, went out, leaving the general engaged in writing. He had been for some time absent, when he hurriedly entered the room.

"I thought it would be so," he observed. "The Lady Superior is about to remove

Miss Maynard to some other establishment, and she will then coolly inform you
that, Sister Clare not being an inmate of
the convent, she cannot be answerable for
her. I learnt this from one of several
people I placed on the watch, and I find
that one of the serving Sisters has come in
to say that a conveyance is wanted immediately at the convent. I have ordered
our carriage, and we will follow the other;
and you can either speak to Miss Maynard as she comes out of the convent, or
meet her at whatever railway station she
goes to."

The general did not quite like this
plan ; he had hoped to see Clara alone,
and be able to speak to her for as long as
might be necessary, so as to convince her
of the fearful mistake she had made,
should she at first show an unwillingness
to leave the convent; still, he had no

other course but to follow Mr. Franklin's advice. They accordingly entered their carriage, and soon overtook another driving in the direction of the convent. At a short distance from it, Mr. Franklin ordered the coachman to pull up, and got out. He and the general then walked leisurely towards the gate, just as they got in sight of which, they caught a glimpse of three muffled figures stepping into the carriage.

"Now is our time," exclaimed Mr. Franklin; "I've bribed the coachman not to move on till I have given him leave, so that should one of those dames prove to be the Lady Superior—and I know her very well—we shall have an opportunity of addressing her; and I think what I say will make her hesitate to use force in preventing Miss Maynard from accompanying you, should you desire her to do so."

The next instant they were alongside the carriage, just as the Lady Superior—for she was one of those inside—had put her head out of the window, peremptorily ordering the coachman to drive on as fast as he could. Though he flourished his whip, he kept his reins tight ; but Mr. Franklin, putting his hand on the door, said, " Madam, my friend General Caulfield, whom I have the honour to introduce to you, desires to have some conversation on a matter of importance with Miss Maynard, and I am glad to see that she is here to answer for herself."

As he spoke, Clara sprang up, and though the Lady Superior and the other Sister attempted to hold her back, she threw herself forward into the general's arms.

" Sister Clare, remember your vow of obedience ; sit quiet, I order you," cried the Lady Superior, in a stern tone; but Clara paid no attention to the command. With an imploring look for protection, she gazed into the general's countenance.

"I wish to accompany you," she whispered; "take me, take me away! don't scold me!"

The general recognised the features of the once bright and blooming girl, though her dress looked strange.

"I have come on purpose to take you, my dear girl," he answered, holding her tightly. "I am in your good father's place—trust to me." He then, turning to the Lady Superior, said, "I have the right, as this young lady's guardian, to take her away from you, as she has expressed her wish to accompany me. Mr. Franklin will explain all that is necessary. I bid you good morning, Madam."

"Sister Clare, remember your vows," again repeated the Lady Superior, in a solemn voice ; "the anathema——"

"I cannot allow such language to be uttered to my client," said Mr. Franklin ; and he went on to explain the legal rights of guardians in a way which was calculated to keep the Lady Superior silent. The general, meantime, half leading, half carrying poor Clara, reached his carriage, which at a sign to the coachman approached to receive them. Mr. Franklin, observing that the general had handed in Clara, followed, having directed the coachman to drive off, leaving the Lady Superior and her companion in a state better imagined than described. Looking back, the lawyer observed that they had re-entered the convent.

Clara was no sooner seated than she burst into tears. "I have been very miserable, but I have myself alone to blame," she said. " I knew what you would think, while I obstinately listened to Mr. and Mrs. Lerew, and to what they had taught Aunt Sarah to say to me. Still, I wanted to consult you, but as you were too angry with me to write, I could not have my doubts solved ; and even Harry cast me off, and refused to have any further correspondence with me. I don't blame him, for I knew his opinions, and he warned me——"

" My dear Clara, do you think it possible that I should not have written to you, or that Harry should have neglected to do so?" interrupted the general. " I wrote letter upon letter, and got no answer, and Harry told me that he had written over and over again, and at last had enclosed a letter to your aunt, but that she had returned it, saying that she did so at the recommendation of your spiritual adviser, who considered that it would be highly improper for you, who had become a bride of the Church, to receive a letter from a mortal lover."

"Then I have been deceived and betrayed," exclaimed Clara, "entirely through my own folly, and I have caused Harry terrible pain and annoyance."

"There is no doubt that you have been deceived and betrayed," said the general; "but we do not blame you, except that instead of seeking guidance and direction from the loving Father who is ever ready to afford it, you allowed yourself to be led by fallible human beings, who in this instance had, I suspect, an object in inducing you to follow the line they had pointed out. You did not distinguish between the works which these Sisters of Charity propose undertaking and the system and principles by which they are guided. The works themselves are such as all Christians are bound to engage in or support, whereas the system is idolatrous, and encourages will-worship; the works are made to support the system, instead of, as it should be, love and obedience to our heavenly Master producing the works. Our loving Father wishes His children to be happy and to enjoy the good things with which He provides them. No monastic rules, no peculiar dress, no vows of obedience to fallible mortals like ourselves, no fasts or penances are required to enable us to obey His laws; all we need is to seek for grace and strength from Him to do His will; and knowing that the blood of Jesus Christ cleanseth from all sin, we can go boldly to Him in prayer, offered up through our sole High Priest and Mediator, who ever pleads the efficacy of that blood."

"I know you speak the truth," said Clara; "but I felt myself so unworthy, I fancied that God would not receive me unless I made some sacrifices in His service."

"You dishonoured Him, my dear child, by thinking so," answered the general; "He will in no wise cast out those who come to Him, and He desires all to come just as they are, with humble and contrite spirits; but not under the idea that they can first put away their sins, and merit His love by any good deeds or penances they may perform. Such acts as are pleasing in His sight must spring from loving obedience to Him; all He does is of free grace; we can merit nothing, because we owe Him everything. When you see this clearly, you will understand more perfectly the wrong principles on which the whole Romish and ritualistic systems, and, believe me, they are identical, are founded."

Through the general's remarks Clara's eyes were quickly opened; it appeared as if a thick veil had been thrown over them, which had suddenly been removed, and she wondered how she could have been so lamentably deceived. She looked upon her convent life, with its rigid rules, its senseless silence, its hours of solitude, its meagre fare, the cold and suffering uselessly endured, its unnatural vigils, its mockeries of religious observances, the cruelties she had seen practised, all tending to depress the spirits and lower the physical powers, with just abhorrence; and then a choking sensation came into her throat, and the colour rose to her cheeks as she thought of the abominable confessional, the questions asked her, and the answers she had had to give. She tried to shut them out from her thoughts. Could she ever be worthy of the pure, honest-minded, open-hearted, noble Harry?

On reaching their sitting-room at the inn, the general looked at Clara's costume.

"I suppose, my dear child, that you would like to assume the ordinary dress of a young lady of the nineneeth century," he said with a smile, "in lieu of those garments of the dark ages."

A smile almost rose to Clara's lips, though her cheeks were blushing and her eyes suffused with tears as she answered, "Yes, I should very much, and I must ask if you will be good enough to send them back to the convent, as they belong to the community, and I have no right to keep them."

"With all imaginable pleasure," exclaimed Mr. Franklin; "and I am happy to say that I can assist you in procuring a desirable costume. I have a relative residing here who is much about your height and figure, and as she has some interest with the mantua-makers, I have no doubt that by to-morrow morning she will induce them to supply you with a travelling-dress and such other articles of apparel as you may require."

Clara expressed her thankfulness, and added, "Pray let it be as simple as possible."

"Oh yes, it shall be such as will become a quakeress if you wish it; I will lose no time about it," said Mr. Franklin, hurrying out of the room.

"Why, he has gone without taking anything to eat; he must be almost starving," observed the general. "I know that I am; and, my dear, I am afraid that you must be hungry, unless you took a late luncheon."

"We had dinner at ten, though I took but little," answered Clara ; "but we are accustomed to go a long time without food."

"Your looks tell me that, my dear," exclaimed the general, ringing the bell. "We must take more care of you in future than you have received lately. I never knew starving enable a person the better to go through the duties of life."

The waiter entered, and the general ordered luncheon to be brought up at once, in a tone which showed that he intended to be obeyed, adding, "Let there be as many delicacies as your cook can provide off-hand."

The lawyer had not returned when luncheon was placed on the table. "Come, my dear, I want to see you do justice to some of these nice things," said the general.

Poor Clara hesitated ; it was a fast-day in the convent—could she at once transgress the rule ? She was going to take simply some bread and preserve, but the general placed a cutlet on her plate. " I must insist on your eating that, and taking a glass or two of good wine to give you strength for your journey to-morrow," he said. Clara had to explain her difficulty.

" I know of no command of the Lord to fast," he observed, " though He stigmatised vain fasts and oblations. The apostles nowhere command it, and the early Christians, until error crept in among them, did not consider fasting a religious duty. In your case let me assure you that it would be a sin to fast when you require your strength restored. You have had much mental trial, and will have more to go through. The mind suffers with the body, and it is your duty to strengthen both. Come, come, eat up the cutlet, and take this glass of sherry."

Clara obeyed, and in a wonderfully short time began to see matters in a brighter light. The general did not fail to explain that one of the great objects of the system from which he wished to emancipate her was that of weakening the minds of those it got into its toils to keep them in subjection. " Such was their aim in insisting on confession, on fasting, and on vigils. What is even a strong man fit for, who is deprived of his sleep and half-starved ? How completely does a man become the slave of the fellow mortal to whom he confides every secret of his heart ! and how much more thoroughly must a weak woman become a slave, who is subjected to the same system ! Add to that the rule of obedience which you tell me is so much insisted on. Obedience to whom ? to a woman as full of faults and weaknesses as other human beings. How sad must be the result! It is terrible to see the name of religion prostituted in such a cause."

Clara ate up the cutlet without any further objection, and meekly submitted to take some of the other delicacies the general placed before her.

" You'll do, my dear," he said, smiling; " we shall have the roses in your cheeks again, I hope, in a few weeks. What I want you to do is to distinguish between God's and man's religions. You have erred from confounding the two. Our loving Father wants a joyous, willing obedience; He allows no one to come between Him and us poor sinners, but our one Mediator and great High Priest, to whom we must confess our sins. He invites us to come direct to Him in prayer. Those dishonour Him who fancy that either ministering angels or departed saints can interfere with our glorious privilege. He who said, ' Rend .your heart, and not your garments,' desires no debasing penances, no fasts, nothing which could weaken the powers of the mind. When you come to look into the subject, you will see that all such practices were invented by the great enemy of souls to draw men off from their reliance on their loving Father, who is ever ready to give grace and help in time of need."

Before luncheon was quite over Mr. Franklin returned. " You will excuse us for not waiting for you," said the general. " Miss Maynard was nearly starving."

" I am glad you did not wait, indeed," answered Mr. Franklin, " for I may com pliment Miss Maynard on looking much better than she did an hour ago. I have

been entirely successful in my mission;
my cousin and her milliner will be here
in a few minutes. I have a message from
my aunt, Mrs. Lawson, who begs that you
and Miss Maynard will stay the night
at her house, as she can there make the
arrangements about her dress with far
more convenience than here."

The general, without stopping to consult Clara, at once accepted the offer.
Clara herself was thankful to move to
a quiet house. Miss Lawson, who was
a sensible girl, understanding Clara's position and feelings, with much thoughtful-
ness made every arrangement she could
require. Having supplied her from her
own wardrobe, she took away the conventual garments, which Mr. Franklin
with infinite satisfaction carefully packed
up and sent with a note, couched in legal
phraseology, to the Lady Superior, re-

questing that Miss Maynard's property might be sent back by return. " I don't suppose we shall get it," he remarked to his cousin ; " but it is as well to see what her ladyship has to say about the matter."

Late in the evening a note arrived from the Lady Superior, who had to assure Mr. Franklin that she possessed nothing belonging to Miss Maynard, who was well aware that any articles brought into the convent became the property of the community, and that all secular dresses were immediately disposed of as useless to those devoted to the service of the Church.

" I call it a perfect swindle," observed Mrs. Lawson,. who was not an admirer of convents. " Miss Maynard tells me she took two trunks full of summer and winter clothing. She had not a notion before she went to the convent how she was to dress or what she was to do."

"I am afraid, notwithstanding, that we cannot indict the Lady Superior as a swindler, whatever opinion we may secretly form of her," answered Mr. Franklin, laughing. "I daresay that Miss Maynard will soon be able to replace her loss. We would rather not have her adventure made public, except for the sake of a warning to others."

Miss Lawson, whose garments fortunately fitted Clara, begged that she would take such as she might require until the dressmaker could forward those which had been ordered. The next morning, heartily thanking Mr. Franklin and his relations, Clara and the general set off for Cheltenham. It was not to be expected that Clara would at once recover her spirits and serenity of mind; but fortunately they had the carriage to themselves, and thus the general had an opportunity of further explaining the subjects he had touched on on the previous day. As he never was without his Bible, he was able to refer to that, and to point to many texts which of late Clara had heard sadly perverted, or which had been carefully avoided. He explained to her the origin of the whole Romish system, and showed her how identical that of the Ritualists was with it ; the great object being to exalt and give power to a priestly caste, who, pretending to stand between God and the sinner, thus obtain power over the minds and property of their fellow-creatures. " Such has been the object of certain men imbued with a desire to rule their more ignorant and more superstitious fellows, from the earliest ages ; it was this spirit which influenced the priests of Egypt, Greece, and Rome ; it exists throughout India, among the savages of America in their medicine - men, in the islands of the Pacific, and indeed in every region of the world. It is the object of the Romish system, and is now exhibiting itself in a more subtle form among the ministers of the Church of England. We properly apply the term sacerdotalism to any system the spirit of which seeks to place a human being in any intermediate character between God and man. Sacerdotalism is in direct opposition and antagonistic to the genius of the Gospel, which enunciates the great truth that there is but one Mediator between God and man, the Man Jesus Christ; that through the atoning blood of Christ, man, if truly turning to Him, and heartily believing, receives directly, and without any other agency whatever, pardon and absolution. He, and He alone, pardoneth and absolveth all them that truly repent, that is, look to Him and unfeignedly believe His holy Gospel. Christ, and Christ alone, is the Way, the Truth, and the Life to seeking, travailing, heavy-laden man ; whereas the Romanists, as do the Ritualists, assert that without the priestly function there is no complete remission, no claim to all the benefit of the Passion, no assurance of God's sanctifying grace. There must be, say these people, contrition, confession, and satisfaction united with the sacerdotal function, a succession of acts, the priest being the organ oj God's sanctifying grace."

" Oh, then, of what mockery, of what sin, have I been guilty ? " exclaimed Clara.

" Turn from it, and look to Jesus, and He grants immediate forgiveness," answered the general.

" Would that all who are misled as

I have been might receive that glorious truth!" cried Clara. "Oh, general, tell it everywhere, and show me how I may help to open the eyes of others as mine have been opened."

"God alone can open the eyes of the blind ; but we can become active instruments in His hands by conveying to them the remedy for their blindness," said the general, taking Clara's hand. "Your words afford me infinite satisfaction, and remove an anxious weight from my heart on your own account, and on that of one naturally still dearer to me. Depend on it that, with God's grace, I will not relax in my efforts to make known the simple Gospel, and to exhibit the sacerdotal system of Rome, and of the so-called ritualism of England, in its true light."

Chapter VI.

ON reaching Cheltenham, the general took Clara to the house of his sister-in-law, a Scotch lady, who received her with the most motherly kindness.

"I very well know the sort of glamour which has been thrown around you, my dear," she said, "so that I can heartily sympathise with you; and I praise God that it has been removed. You can now therefore look with confidence for grace and strength from Him who is the giver of all good, to walk forward in the enjoyment of that true happiness which God in His mercy affords to His creatures. There is abundance of work for our sex, which can be carried out in a straightforward, Protestant, English fashion."

"I shall be thankful to find it," said Clara.

"You will not have long to wait, my dear," answered Mrs. Caulfield; "but at present you require being nursed yourself: you must let me take you in hand."

As soon as the general had deposited Clara with his sister-in-law, he set off and paid his promised visit to Mary Lennard. On reaching Mrs. Barnett's establishment, he was shown into a handsome drawing-room, where that lady soon presented herself, under the belief that he had come to place a daughter with her. She bowed gracefully as she glided into a seat, and smilingly enquired the object of his visit.

"I have come to see Miss Mary Lennard, daughter of my particular friend, the Reverend John Lennard," answered he.

"She is too ill, I regret to say, to see visitors," answered the schoolmistress. "Had her father come, I of course should not have objected."

"I am acting in the place of her father," said the general, "and I must insist on seeing the young lady, who has, I understand, been made ill by a system of fasting and penances which all right-minded people must consider objectionable."

"Sir, you astonish me," exclaimed Mrs. Barnett. "I should suppose that every clergyman would wish his daughter to fast on Fridays and other days ordered by the Church; and with regard to penances, such have been imposed by the priest to whom she has duly gone to confession."

"Why, I thought this was a Protestant school," exclaimed the general, astonished.

"That term I repudiate," answered the lady. "I am a daughter of the Anglican Church, and as such I wish to bring up all my pupils."

"You may act according to your conscience, but parents may differ from you as to whether you are right in compelling growing children to fast, as also in allowing them to confess to a person whom you call a priest," answered the general. "I regret having to act in any way which is disagreeable to you, but I must insist, madam, with the authority given me by Mr. Lennard, on seeing his daughter alone, and judging what steps I shall take."

The lady hesitated; the general put Mr. Lennard's letter into her hand. She still hesitated.

"Have you any reason for wishing me not to see Mary?" he asked.

"She may appear worse than she really is," said Mrs. Barnett. "Our medical attendant has visited her daily."

"That makes it more necessary for me to see her and judge for myself," said the general, in a firm tone.

Mrs. Barnett rang the bell, and a servant appearing, she told her to inform Miss Lennard that a friend of her father wished to see her.

"She isn't able to get up, marm, I'm afraid," was the answer.

"Then show me her room," said the general, rising; and without waiting to hear Mrs. Barnett's remarks, he followed the servant, who led the way upstairs to a room containing four beds. A cough struck his ears as he entered. On one of the beds lay poor Mary; her once rosy cheek was pale and thin, and her large eyes unusually bright. She knew him at once, and stretching out both her hands, said, "I am glad to see you; but I thought papa would come."

The general explained that Mr. Lennard was prevented from doing what he wished.

"Then, will you take me away from this?" she asked, in a whisper; "I am sure that papa would do so. I am not happy here; but do not let Mrs. Barnett know I said so."

"If you can be removed without risk, I certainly will take you," answered the general.

"Oh, yes, yes! I shall be well soon. I could get up now if they will give me my clothes," exclaimed Mary.

The day was bright and warm; and as the general felt sure that Mary could be removed without danger, he determined to take her to his sister-in-law's immediately.

"Take me! take me!" said Mary; "I feel quite strong enough, and the doctor said that there was nothing particularly the matter with me."

Her eagerness to go was still further increased when she heard that she was to be taken care of by Clara Maynard.

"I thought that she had been shut up in a convent," she exclaimed. "The girls here were saying that it is a very holy life, though I don't know that there are many who wish to lead it; but I was very, very sorry to hear of Clara's being a nun, because I thought that perhaps I might never see her again, and of all people I wondered that she should turn nun."

"I trust that she has given up all intention of becoming one," said the general; "but you will see her soon, and she will tell you what she thinks about the matter."

The general then told the servant to assist Miss Lennard in dressing, while he went out to obtain a conveyance. On returning to the house, he desired again to see Mrs. Barnett. The lady was somewhat indignant, and warned him that he must be responsible for the consequences of removing Miss Lennard.

"Of course I am, and I am taking her where she can be more carefully nursed than is possible in a school," answered the general.

Mary was soon ready, and her box packed up. The thoughts of going away restored her strength, and she walked downstairs without difficulty. The general carefully wrapped her up, and telling her to keep the shawl over her head and mouth, lifted her into the carriage. They had but a short distance to go. Clara was delighted to find that Mary was to remain; but on perceiving how ill the poor girl evidently was, she felt very sad. Mary was, however, not at all the worse for being removed, and Mrs. Caulfield immediately sent for her own medical man to see her. He looked very grave, but gave no decided opinion. "She has been poorly fed, and her mind overtaxed for one so young," he remarked. "We must see what proper care and nourishment will effect; but I must not disguise from you that I am anxious about her."

Clara begged that Mary might be placed in her bed, while she occupied a small camp-bed at its foot.

"But you will have no room to turn," observed Mrs. Caulfield.

"It is wider and far softer than the

one to which I have been accustomed," she answered, smiling, " and I shall be much happier to be near Mary than away from her."

Clara had now ample occupation in attending on her sick friend, though Mrs. Caulfield insisted on her driving out every day, and advised her to receive the visits of several friends who called. With the consciousness that she was of essential use to Mary, her own spirits returned and her health improved. The rest of her time was spent in working, or reading to Mary, or playing and singing to her. The healthy literature the general procured for Mary benefited Clara as much as it did her friend; it was an invigorating change from the monastic legends and similar works which were alone allowed to be perused in the convent. She thought it better not to say much about

her own life there ; but Mary was not so
reticent with regard to her school existence.

"The only books allowed to be read
were those written by priests, ritualists,
or Roman Catholics. "The books were
mostly very dull," said Mary; "but as we
had no others, we were glad to get them.
Then a clergyman came, who told us that
we were all very sinful, but that when we
came to him at confession he would give
us absolution ; and as we thought that
very nice, we did as he advised us ; but
I did not at all like the questions he put ;
some of them were dreadful, and I know
he said the same to the other girls. Still,
as we were kept very strict in school, we
were glad to get out to church as often as
we could ; there was the walk, which was
pleasant in fine weather ; and then we
could look at the people who were there,
and the music was often very fine, and

the sermon was never very long; and sometimes the young gentlemen used to come and sit near us, and talk to the elder girls when no one was looking—at least, we thought they were young gentlemen, but, as it turned out, they were anything but such. One of them, especially, used to give notes to one of the girls, and she wrote others in return, and we thought it very romantic, and of course no one would tell Mrs. Barnett of it. At last, one day, we thought that the girl had gone into confession; but instead of joining us she slipped out of the church at a side door, where her lover was waiting to receive her. Away they went by the train to a distance, where they were married, and could not be found for some time. At last they came back, when it was discovered that the young man was the son of a small tradesman in the place, though he had pretended that he had a good fortune and excellent prospects. Mrs. Barnett was horrified, and tried to hush matters up, and I believe the parents of the girl did not like to expose her for their own sakes. I know that I and the rest were very wrong in our behaviour, and I will not excuse myself, except to say that everything was done to make us hypocrites. Religion was very much talked about on Sundays and saints' days; but I have learnt more of the Gospel since I came here, from you and dear General Caulfield, than I ever knew before."

Clara sighed as she thought how little she herself had known till lately.

"You had better not talk any more about your school," she said; "let us speak rather about what we read, and things of real importance."

Clara had become very much alarmed about Mary. Wholesome and regular food, and gentle exercise in the carriage when the weather was fine, somewhat restored her strength ; but there was the hectic spot on her cheek, and the brightness of the eyes, which too surely told of consumption. Mr. Lennard at length arrived; he looked much depressed, and was shocked at seeing the change in his daughter. He had a most unsatisfactory account to give of his son, whom he had searched for for some time in vain. At last he discovered that the young gentleman had been formally received into the Romish Church, and that his friend the priest was concealing him somewhere in London. The poor father found out where his son was through a letter which was forwarded from Luton, in which the youth asked for a remittance for his support, as he had expended all his means, and could not longer, he observed, encroach on the limited stipend of his friend, Father Lascelles. Mr. Lennard, still hoping that it might be possible to win back the youth, wrote entreating him to return home, and on his declining to do this, he offered to let him continue his course at Oxford, that he might fit himself for entering one of the learned professions. After a delay of two or three days, Alfred wrote saying that he had applied to his bishop, who would not consent to his doing so, and that as he was now under his spiritual guidance, he must obey him rather than a heretic father.

"You will pardon me for calling you so," continued Master Alfred ; "but while you remain severed from the one true Church, such you must be in the eyes of all Catholics, one of whom I have become."

"I was too much grieved to laugh, as I might otherwise have done, at the boy's impertinence," observed Mr. Lennard to the general ; "but as I look upon him as deceived by artful men, I cannot treat him with the rigour he deserves. What do you recommend, general ? "

"We must, if possible, get him to come home, and then put the truth clearly before him," remarked the general.

"I am afraid that I cannot say enough to induce him to change," said Mr. Lennard, with a deep sigh.

"We must have recourse, whatever we do, to earnest prayer," observed the general. "I cannot suppose that your son's mind is already so completely per- verted as to be impregnable to the truth."

"Alas, it is not for so short a time," answered Mr. Lennard ; "the seed was sown by the tutor with whom he spent a

year or more, and finally matured by this
same Father Lascelles and his tutor at
college. He is the very man with whom
Mr. Lerew read, I find. I wonder that he
was not the means of his older pupil's
perversion."

"Mr. Lerew is not so honest a man as
your son," answered the general; "Mr.
Lerew was about to take orders, and
would prove a useful tool, while it was
more prudent to secure your son at once,
as he, it was supposed, would inherit your
property. I wish that I could offer you
consolation; but I fear that you would
consider me a Job's comforter at the
best."

Mr. Lennard had come hoping to take
Mary home; but she appeared scarcely
able to undertake so long a journey, and
Clara confessed that she herself was un
willing to return as yet to Luton. Poor

Mr. Lennard was nearly heart-broken on hearing from the doctor that he thought very badly of Mary's case.

"Could I not take her abroad, to Madeira, or the south of France ? " he asked.

"It would be, I feel confident, useless," was the melancholy answer; "had she strength to stand the journey, her life might possibly be prolonged for a few weeks; but she would probably lose more by the exertion of travelling than she would gain by the change. Here she is under loving care, and we may alleviate her sufferings."

Some more weeks wore by, and Mary grew worse. Mr. Lennard felt, what some parents do not, that it was his duty, though a painful one, to tell his daughter that her days were numbered, and at the same time to afford her such comfort as, according to his knowledge, he could. He gently broke the subject.

" I know it," she answered. " I asked Clara if she thought I was dying, and she told me that the doctor said I could not recover; but, dear papa, I am prepared to go away to One who loves me, though I am sorry, very sorry, to leave you, and Clara, and the general, and those who have been kind to me."

The tears were falling from Mr. Len nard's eyes.

" You have been a dear good girl, and have enjoyed the blessing of baptism, and have been confirmed, and have received the sacrament; you shall receive it again if you wish, and I hope that God will take you to heaven."

" Oh, dear, dear papa, don't speak so," answered Mary; " I know that I am a wretched sinner; I have done nothing to.

merit God's love and mercy; but I know that Jesus Christ died for me, and that His blood cleanseth from all sin ; and, trusting to Him, I am sure that He will receive me in the place He has gone before to prepare for those who love Him. I have faith in Christ ; that is my happiness, hope, and confidence. I am not afraid to die, for I know that He will be with me through the shadow of the valley of death."

Mr. Lennard gazed at her, unable to speak. He could not ask her further questions, but was revolving in his own mind the meaning of what she had said. She had no confidence in any of the objects which he had been accustomed to present to the minds of the dying, if he believed them to be good Churchmen, and if not, he had always urged them to repent of their sins and to take the sacrament, in the hope that thus God might receive them into heaven. Mary's remarks had brought new light to his soul; she trusted solely to the *all-finished work* of Christ, to whom she looked as her Saviour, with full assurance that He would welcome her to heaven. She thought not, she spoke not, of any of the rites and ceremonies in which he had trusted himself, and had taught others to trust, rather than to the blood of the Atonement. She did not ask even him, her father, and, as he had fancied himself, a priest, to offer a prayer on her behalf. No, she was resting joyfully on Christ as her all-sufficient Saviour.

"I see it all now," he said, half aloud; "it is this of which the general has been speaking to me lately, but which I did not comprehend."

"Yes, dear papa; Jesus did it all long

ago ; He saved me then, and I am trusting in Him ; that makes me so happy, so very happy," exclaimed Mary.

"I believe as you do," answered Mr. Lennard ; "would that I had known and taught your poor brother the same truth ! it would have prevented him from falling into the toils of Rome."

"We can pray for him, that he may be rescued from them," said Mary.

"I wished to make him a sound Churchman, and taught him that there is but one true Church, and that that is the Church of England ; and miserable has been the result," said Mr. Lennard.

"Alfred may be brought back. God will hear our united prayers," whispered Mary.

"I cannot pray with faith that my prayer will be answered," he murmured. "I did my utmost to instil the belief into him, and he has ever since been with those who have done their utmost to forward the same notion."

Mary now became her father's comforter. She lingered with those who loved her for some time longer, proving an especial blessing to Clara, who had, as her ever-watchful nurse, constant employment and occupation for her thoughts and feelings. The general remained with his sister, and afforded Clara that instruction and guidance she so much needed, while he put into her hands such books as were best calculated to strengthen her mind and to do away with all traces of that mysticism which she had imbibed both before and during her life in the convent. With clearer perceptions of truth than she had ever before enjoyed, she was now better able to perform her duties in life. She had written to her aunt, saying that she hoped some day to return home, but was at present employed in nursing her young friend Mary Lennard, whom she could not at present leave ; but she did not think it necessary to speak of her escape from the convent, or to enter into other particulars, so that Miss Pemberton remained in ignorance of her change of opinions.

Mr. Lennard had twice gone away in the hope of meeting his son and inducing him to attend the death-bed of his sister; but the priests, who were well informed of the religious opinions of those who had taken charge of Mary, made him send various excuses, and poor Mary was deprived of the satisfaction of seeing her brother again. When Mr. Lennard returned, Mary had become much weaker, and she could only whisper, "Pray for poor Alfred ; don't be angry with him—

he may be brought back;" and her young spirit went to be with the Saviour in whom she trusted. Clara aided the general in comforting their friend.

The bereaved father found peace at last; but often before that, in the bitterness of his heart, he would exclaim, "It was that school, that abominable system of fasting and penance, and that accursed confessional, which killed her; and to have my poor weak misguided boy carried off and enslaved body and soul by those wolves in sheep's clothing, it is more than I can bear! It was I—I alone, who in my blindness and ignorance and folly exposed them to the malign influences which have caused their destruction. I have been the murderer of my children!"

A few days after Mary's funeral, Clara, with the general and Mr. Lennard, returned to Luton. Miss Pemberton received her niece with a look of astonishment.

"Why, I expected to see you dressed as a nun, Clara," she exclaimed; "have you given up your vocation? Dear me! Mr. Lerew will be very much disappointed; he fully expected that you would devote your fortune to St. Agatha's."

"I will explain matters to you, aunt, by-and-by," answered Clara, not wishing on her first arrival at home to enter into any discussion. "I hope that you have not felt yourself very solitary during my long absence."

"As to that, I can't say I have been very lively, for the whole neighbourhood is divided, and because I go to church and confession, all of your father's old friends have ceased to call on me; but of late I have begun to think that they are not altogether wrong. I must acknowledge that since Sir Reginald and Lady Bygrave, and Mrs. Lerew, and two or three other people turned Catholics, my confidence in the vicar and the High Church has been a little shaken. Mrs. Lerew wanted me to turn too; but I was not going to do that, and even the vicar did not advise it, though he said he couldn't help his wife going over ; for if so many went, people's suspicions would be aroused, and he should be unable to establish his college."

"I am truly thankful that you did not go over," answered Clara. "I have learnt a good deal about the Ritualists of late, and I am very sure that their tendency is towards Rome. I have one favour to ask, that is, should Mr. Lerew call, that you will not admit him, as it would be painful to me to see him again, for I cannot receive him as a friend."

"Why, have you found out anything about him?" asked Miss Pemberton, her conscience accusing her.

"There is much, aunt, to which I object in him," answered Clara, firmly.

"Well, I don't wish you to be annoyed, my dear, in any way," said Miss Pemberton; "and, in truth, I suspect that he wanted to get hold of your fortune for his new college. If he finds that he has no chance of that, I don't think he will trouble you much."

"I would rather not think about him in any way," said Clara; "and do pray tell me how Widow Jones and Mrs. Humble and her blind daughter, and the poor Hobbies, with their idiot boy, are getting on. I must go and see them and my other friends as soon as possible."

"Clara then went on to make further enquiries about her poorer neighbours, and was grieved to find that her aunt had not troubled herself about them during her absence.

"It was all my fault," she said to herself; "I was placed here to help them, and I have neglected that very clear duty by giving way to delusive fancies."

Clara lost no time in carrying out her intentions, and was received with a hearty welcome wherever she went. Very frequently remarks were made which showed her that the poor had a clearer perception of the tendencies of the ritualistic system than she herself had previously possessed.

"We be main glad to see you again looking so like yourself, Miss," exclaimed Dame Hobby. "They said as how the vicar had got you to go into a monkery that he might spend your money to pay for his fripperies in the church, his candles, and that smoky stuff, and his pictures and gold-embroidered dresses, and flags and crosses, and all they singing men and women, and dressing up the little boys, as if God cared for such things, or they could make us love Him and serve Him better, for that's my notion of what religion should do. The Bible says we can go straight to God through Jesus Christ, and pray to Him as our Father; and all these things seem to me only to stand in the way; and when we want to be praying, we are instead looking about at the goings on, and listening to the music. 'Tisn't that I haven't a respect for the parson and the church; but when I go to church, I go to pray and to hear God's word read and explained from the pulpit in a way simple people can understand."

Clara found much the same opinions expressed by all she visited. The general

came every day to see her, to strengthen
and support her. His conversation had
a very good effect on Miss Pemberton,
whose eyes having once been opened
to the tendencies of the ritualistic
system, she was enabled to see it in
its true light. She resolved to have
nothing more to say to Mr. Lerew, and
to refuse to receive him, should he call.
Soon after Clara returned home he had
started on a tour to collect funds for
his college, and as he was absent, Clara
was saved from the annoyance she had
expected. The general was fortunately
paying a visit to Clara and her aunt when
Mr. Lerew at length came to call on
Miss Pemberton to enquire why she had
not during his absence attended church.
It was agreed that it would be better to
admit him. He tried to assume his usual
unimpassioned manner as he entered the

room; but the frown on his brow and his puckered lips showed his annoyance and anger. He had not had the early training which enables the Jesuit priest effectually to conceal his feelings. He had evidently heard that Clara had left the convent, as he showed no surprise at seeing her. He probably would have behaved very differently to what he did, had not the general been present. Shaking hands with all the party, he took a seat, and brushing his hat with his glove, cleared his throat, and then said, " I was afraid, Miss Pemberton, that you were ill, as you have not, I understand, favoured the church with your presence for the last two Sundays."

" I had my reasons for not going," answered Miss Pemberton ; " and I may as well tell you that I purpose in future not to attend your church, as I see clearly that your preaching and the system carried on there leads Romeward; and I have no wish to become a Romanist or to encourage others by my presence to run the risk of becoming so either."

"Romanist! Romanist!" exclaimed Mr. Lerew; "I have no dealings with Rome; I don't want my people to become Romanists."

"The proof of the pudding is in the eating, Mr. Lerew," answered Miss Pemberton, dryly. "I have expressed my resolution, and I hope to adhere to it."

Mr. Lerew was not prepared with an answer; but turning to Clara, he said, "I trust, Miss Maynard, that though you have thought fit to abandon the sacred calling to which I had hoped you would have devoted yourself, you will still remain faithful to the Church."

"I cannot make any promise on the

subject," answered Clara, being anxious not to say anything to irritate the vicar. "I believe that I was before blinded and led away from the truth, when I was induced to enter the sisterhood of St. Barbara, and I now desire to retrieve my error."

"I understand you, ladies," exclaimed the vicar, losing command of his temper. "Remember that by deserting the Church you are guilty of the heinous crime of schism, for which, till repented of, there is no pardon here or hereafter. General Caulfield, I fear that you have much to answer for in having set the example in my parish; you will excuse me for saying so."

"It is you and those who side with you who are guilty of the schism of which you speak," said the general, mildly. "The Church of England protests clearly against the errors of Rome; and you, by adopting many, if not all those errors, are virtually cutting yourself off from that Church, although you retain a post in it. But let me explain that the schism spoken of in the New Testament is the departing from the truth of the Gospel, and the practices it inculcates; in other words, those who leave Christ's spiritual Church. My great object is to draw my fellow-creatures into that Church; to induce them to accept Christ as the Way, the Truth, and the Life; to persuade them to grasp that hand so lovingly stretched forth to lead them to the Father. I ignore the schism of which you speak, invented by the sacerdotalists to alarm the uneducated. You have my reply, Mr. Lerew, and I wish you clearly to understand that I purpose, with God's assistance, by every means in my power to make known the truth of the Gospel in this parish and in every place where false teaching prevails."

"Then I shall look upon you as a schismatic and a foe to our Church," exclaimed Mr. Lerew, rising.

"I have already explained to you the true meaning of schism," said the general, quietly, "and have particularly to request that all further discussion on this subject may cease. Miss Pemberton and her niece have expressed their sentiments, and you have long known mine. I trust that none of us will change; and anything further said on the subject can only cause annoyance."

Mr. Lerew saw that he had lost his influence over Clara and her aunt, and not wishing to remain longer than he could help in the general's society, quickly took his departure. He had not as yet seen

Mr. Lennard since his return, nor had he heard the cause of poor Mary's death ; he at once drove over to his house. Instead of the hearty manner Mr. Lennard usually exhibited, he received his visitor with marked coldness. Mr. Lerew was puzzled.

"I am sorry that my absence from home has prevented me hitherto from calling on you," he said ; "but I rejoice to have you back, and I hope that you will assist at the celebrations in my church."

"I come to a sad home, deprived of my young daughter by death, and my son by his perversion to the Church of Rome," answered Mr. Lennard, gravely, not noticing the last remark. "I know that my child has left this world for a far better ; but I cannot forget that the seeds of her disease were produced by the system practised at the school you recommended, Mr. Lerew, as also that my son's perversion was much owing to the instruction received from the tutor under whom, by your advice, I placed him. The daughter of my late friend Captain Maynard has happily escaped from the toils you threw around her; and though I am ready heartily to forgive the injuries you have inflicted on me, I feel myself called on to expose the traitorous efforts you and others with whom you are associated are making to uproot the Protestant principles of the Church. I believe that I am actuated by no hostile feeling towards yourself personally; but I will take every means in my power to put a stop to the practices which you pursue in your church."

"You acknowledge yourself, then, an enemy to me and to the Church!" exclaimed Mr. Lerew, who felt braver in the

presence of Mr. Lennard, whom he considered a weak man, than he had in
that of General Caulfield.

" I desire not to be an enemy to you
personally," answered Mr. Lennard, mildly ;
" but to your system, which is calculated
to lead your flock fearfully astray, I am,
and trust I shall ever remain, an invete-
rate foe."

In vain did Mr. Lerew endeavour to
win back his former dupe. Mr. Lennard
had clearly seen the chasm which divides
the Protestant Church of England from
the Romish system and its counterpart,
Ritualism, and, as an honest man, he was
not to be drawn over. Again defeated,
the vicar of Luton-cum-Crosham had to
take his departure. He still, however,
found dupes to subscribe sufficient funds
for the establishment of his college, and a
Lady Superior of high ritualistic proclivi-

ties to take charge of it, and masters who, provided they got their stipends, cared nothing about the object of the institution. By putting out his candles and omitting some of the ceremonies at his church whenever the bishop or rural dean came to visit it, he was able to retain his living. By means of a plausible prospectus, he, with other ritualistic brethren, induced the parents and guardians of a number of young ladies, tempted by the moderate expense and advantages offered, to send them to the college, where, with the usual superficial accomplishments they received, their minds were thoroughly imbued with ritualistic principles. General Caulfield and Mr. Lennard prevented several of their friends from being thus taken in. A good many people were staggered when they heard that the vicar's wife and his patrons—Lady Bygrave and Sir Reginald

—had become Romanists. They had all three lately set off for Rome itself, under the escort of the Abbé Hénon. They were there received with due honour by the Pope, and had the satisfaction of hearing from the infallible lips of his Holiness that England would, ere long, be won from the power of the infidel Protestants, and restored to the bosom of the Catholic Church ; and believing themselves to be not the least important members of the British race, they returned home to spread the joyful intelligence among those who were ready to believe them. The chapel erected in their park had almost as large a congregation as that of the parish church, especially as winter approached, and blankets and coals were liberally distributed among the worshippers.

Clara, meantime, had pursued the even tenor of her way. Her aunt was greatly changed for the better ; she had become kind and considerate to her, and frequently accompanied her in her visits among the poor and suffering in the wide district she had taken under her charge. Though Clara generally drove in her pony-carriage, she occasionally, when the distance was not too great, went on foot. She had one day thus gone out, carrying a basket stored with delicacies for several sick people, when, as she was proceeding along a sheltered lane, overhung with trees, she heard a quick footstep behind her. She turned her head and saw Harry. Her first impulse was to rush towards him— then for a moment she stopped. He held out his arms.

" Can you forgive me for my folly, and the pain and grief I have caused you ? " she exclaimed.

" I have forgotten it all in the happi-

ness of seeing you thus employed, exactly as I should wish," he answered ;
" never let us speak about it ; my father
has told me all. You were ever dear to
me, even when I thought that I had lost
you. You have learned to distinguish the
true from the false, and I shall never for
a moment, in future, have the slightest
fear that, seeking for guidance from above,
you will mistake the one for the other.

THE END.

Hazell, Watson, and Viney, Printers, London and Aylesbury.

TOSSED ON THE WAVES. By EDWIN HODDER, Author of "The Junior Clerk," etc.

"Will rank with the best of story books for boys. It has some good schoolboy experience, and is a capital sea tale. The best feature of the book, however, is its manly religiousness, illustrated by some well-defined characters. We have thoroughly enjoyed reading this."—NONCONFORMIST.

ROBERT RAIKES, *Journalist and Philanthropist.* A History of the Origin of Sunday Schools. By A. GREGORY.

MARINER NEWMAN; *or, a Voyage in the Good Ship "Glad Tidings" to the Promised Land.* By the Rev. DUNCAN MACGREGOR.

FOURTH THOUSAND.

CHILDREN RECLAIMED FOR LIFE: *the Story of Dr. Barnardo's Work in London.* By the Author of the "Romance of the Streets," etc. With full-page Illustrations.

"The story of the experiences met with in the work of gathering these outcasts together is profoundly interesting. What could be more pathetic, for instance, than the history of a poor little 'waif' who was known by the comic soubriquet of 'carrots'?"—SPECTATOR.

A NEW ILLUSTRATED EDITION OF

TAYLOR'S HYMNS FOR INFANT MINDS. Containing twenty-six choice Engravings from designs by JOSIAH GILBERT, Author of "Cadore; or, Titian's Country;" etc.

"In addition to fine toned paper and clear type are twenty-eight exquisite illustrations, with one or two exceptions, original. Mr. Gilbert's professional reputation as an artist is very high—but neither in conceptive drawings nor execution has he, we think, ever surpassed these delicate and picturesque drawings. It is a little gem of a book.'—BRITISH QUARTERLY REVIEW.